P9-BAT-539

newcharlie

I called him Newcharlie because Rahway hadn't sent the guy I remembered home. This guy standing at the mirror moving his hair around his head was someone—some*thing*—different.

Right after he came home from Rahway, I got up in the middle of the night to look at him. He'd been away for more than two years, and the guy sleeping across from me was a stranger. Some days he'd just sit on that bed with his hands hanging down between his knees. Just staring out the window and looking evil. But when he was asleep, his face spread out—all the frowns and scowls just kind of faded and he looked like Charlie again, ready to care about something, to be happy, or to cry about stray animals.

Newcharlie checked himself out for a moment without saying anything. He's light brown with thick black eyebrows and Mama's nose. He winked at himself, then caught me watching him in the mirror and gave me the finger. I looked away from him without giving him the finger back.

What changed you, Cha? I wanted to ask him. *What made you cold?*

ALSO BY JACQUELINE WOODSON

After Tupac and D Foster

Behind You

Beneath a Meth Moon

Between Madison and Palmetto

Brown Girl Dreaming

The Dear One

Feathers

From the Notebooks of Melanin Sun

The House You Pass on the Way

Hush

I Hadn't Meant to Tell You This

If You Come Softly

Last Summer with Maizon

Lena

Locomotion

Maizon at Blue Hill

Peace, Locomotion

JACQUELINE WOODSON

miracle's boys

PUFFIN BOOKS
An Imprint of Penguin Group (USA)

PUFFIN BOOKS
Published by the Penguin Group
Penguin Group (USA) LLC
375 Hudson Street
New York, New York 10014

USA * Canada * UK * Ireland * Australia
New Zealand * India * South Africa * China

penguin.com
A Penguin Random House Company

First published in the United States of America by G. P. Putnam's Sons,
a division of Penguin Young Readers Group, 2000
This edition published by Puffin Books, a division of Penguin Young Readers Group, 2010

Copyright © 2000 by Jacqueline Woodson

Penguin supports copyright. Copyright fuels creativity, encourages diverse voices,
promotes free speech, and creates a vibrant culture. Thank you for buying an authorized
edition of this book and for complying with copyright laws by not reproducing, scanning,
or distributing any part of it in any form without permission. You are supporting writers
and allowing Penguin to continue to publish books for every reader.

THE LIBRARY OF CONGRESS HAS CATALOGED THE G. P. PUTNAM'S SONS EDITION AS FOLLOWS:
Woodson, Jacqueline.
Miracle's boys / Jacqueline Woodson
p. cm.
Summary: Twelve-year-old Lafayette's close relationship with his older brother
Charlie changes after Charlie is released from a detention home and blames
Lafayette for the death of their mother.
ISBN: 978-0-399-23113-1 (hc)
[1. Brothers—Fiction. 2. Family problems—Fiction. 3. Orphans—Fiction.
4. Racially mixed people—Fiction. 5. School—Fiction.]
I. Title.
PZ7.W868 Mi 2000 [Fic]—dc21 99-040050

Puffin Books ISBN 978-0-14-241553-5

Printed in the United States of America

15 17 19 20 18 16 14

For Nicolas

miracle's boys

ONE

"BROTHERS IS THE BADDEST. THEN COMES DO-
minicans. Dominicans don't mess around. I'm cool
with Dominicans though. They don't mess with me, I
don't mess with them."

I lay back on my bed and listened to my brother
Newcharlie talking. We had shared this room since the
day I was born. And I swear since the day I was born,
he'd been going on about who was the baddest. Used
to be Puerto Ricans were the second baddest, but
somewhere along the road their status dropped. Brothers were always at the top or the next ones down.

1

Newcharlie wasn't talking to me. Since he'd gotten home from Rahway Home for Boys a few months ago, he never talked to me. He was combing his hair and talking to Aaron. They'd known each other forever to say "W's up" and stuff, but they didn't start hanging till Newcharlie came home from Rahway. Seems once Newcharlie saw the inside of Rahway, most of the guys around here who cut school, hung out real late, and got into all kinds of stuff thought he was some kind of wonderful. Aaron acted like he wanted to kiss the heels of Newcharlie's shoes, hanging on to Newcharlie's words like they were something special. And Newcharlie was just as stupid over Aaron. Hanging out with him like Aaron was his brother. Like Aaron was me.

Newcharlie and Aaron were the same height and walked the same way, and now they had the same meanness. Aaron's meanness had always been around him. Even when we were small, we'd walk past him and he'd say something negative. Like when Mama used to make us go to church on Sundays. We'd be all dressed up walking to the bus stop, and Aaron'd say something like "Mama's church boys going to meet their maker." Or the time our big brother, Ty'ree, stopped him from snatching this little kid's Halloween bag. Aaron didn't take the bag, but he kept glaring over his shoulder as me and Ty'ree and the kid walked away, saying, "That's all right, church boy. That's all right." Like he had something waiting for us later on. Newcharlie's meanness was as new as his name. He'd come back from Rahway with it, and the way he and Aaron hung so tight, you'd think he didn't remember those days when we crossed to the other side of the street when we saw Aaron and his boys hanging out.

I watched Newcharlie part his hair on the side and comb it one way, then shake his head, part it on the other, and pull the comb through it again. His hair's curly, like our mama's was—jet-black curls that girls go crazy for. He's three years older than me but only a little bit taller, and at the rate he was going school-wise, come this time next year, I'd be almost caught up with him. I'd just started seventh grade and Newcharlie was repeating ninth, but he didn't seem to care one way or the other.

The *old Charlie* would have cared about me catching up to him. He would have sat down at the dining-room table and crammed, because he would have been embarrassed about me being in almost the same grade as him. See, the old Charlie had feelings. If Charlie saw a stray cat or dog, he'd start crying. Not out-and-out bawling, but he'd just see it and start tearing up. Sometimes, when we were out walking, he'd turn away real fast and I'd know it was because he saw the shadow of some stray animal and was wishing it wasn't out in the cold. Once he told me that some nights he lay in bed just praying for all the stray animals out there. *There's a lot of them, you know,* Charlie said. *And probably not a whole lot of people praying for them.* He told me about St. Francis of Assisi, how he was the guy who looked out for all the animals. He said him and St. Francis were the only two asking God to help those animals walking the cold streets not to freeze to death. I promised Charlie I'd pray too.

And sometimes, late at night, Charlie would just start talking, telling me stories about how things were before I was born—memories of him and our older brother, Ty'ree, and my mama and daddy together. Wasn't ever anything mean in it—like that he wished I hadn't been born or something—just stories, quiet stories that would make me smile and help me fall asleep.

Now I called him Newcharlie because Rahway hadn't sent the guy I was just talking about home. This guy standing at the mirror moving his hair around his head was someone—some*thing*—different. Not the guy who used to laugh and tell jokes and put his arm around my shoulder. This guy never did any of those things. Ever.

Right after he came home from Rahway, I got up in the middle of the night to look at him. He'd been away for more than two years, and the guy sleeping across from me was a stranger. Some days he'd just sit on that bed with his hands hanging down between his knees. Just staring out the window and looking evil. But when he was asleep, his face spread out—all the frowns and scowls just kind of faded and he looked like Charlie again, ready to care about something, to be happy, or to cry about stray animals.

Newcharlie checked himself out for a moment without saying anything. He's light brown with thick black eyebrows and Mama's nose. He winked at himself, then caught me watching him in the mirror and gave me the finger. I looked away from him without giving him the finger back.

What changed you, Cha? I wanted to ask him. What made you cold?

"Ya'll don't go to church no more?" Aaron nosed.

I swallowed and caught Newcharlie's eye. He looked back at me for a second, then frowned.

"Church is for little boys," he said. "Little mama's boys. I look like a little mama's boy to you?"

Aaron shrugged.

The last time any of us was in a church was for Mama's funeral. I didn't want to see the inside of one again. Least not for a long time. Least till the thought of even *passing* by one isn't enough to make me choke up and start bawling about Mama.

"Stupid little mama's boys like Lala," Newcharlie said.

"My name ain't Lala," I said.

In the summer I go down south to my great-aunt Cecile's house. If the watermelons are ripe, she'll buy one. When we get home, she always takes it out back and breaks it open against a rock, then scoops out the heart of it—the sweetest, reddest part—and hands it to me. I stared out the window. Somebody had done that to Charlie. Scooped out his heart and sent the empty bitter rind of him on home.

Aaron was sitting on the bed directly across from mine, Newcharlie's bed, and he was rolling one of his pants legs up real slowly. Sometimes when he looked at me, I felt the coldness, like somebody was dripping ice water down my back.

"Anyway, Puerto Ricans," Newcharlie said. "If they're in a gang, then you got a problem. But if they're on their own, then it's cool. Most of the ones in Rahway had gangs behind them."

"I don't know no Puerto Ricans that ain't in a gang, Cha," Aaron said.

"What're you talking 'bout?" I said. "We're half Puerto Rican and we ain't in no gang, and you're all Puerto Rican and you ain't either."

"How you know what I'm in with your little self?" Aaron said. "You don't know nothing about me, little boy."

Aaron looked me up and down like he was looking at something that didn't even have a right to be in the world. He was wearing a Yankees baseball cap with the front of it pulled down over his eyes so that he had to lift his whole face to look at me. I thought that was a stupid way to wear a hat but didn't say anything about it.

"I don't know what my size got to do with anything, but I know you ain't in no—"

"Mind your business, Lala." Newcharlie glared at me through the mirror. "Nobody in this room talking to you. You hear anybody call your name? When somebody calls your name, then somebody's talking to you, and nobody in this room is *ever* gonna be calling your name."

"So just keep your stupid mouth closed," Aaron said, "and maybe you'll live."

"Lafayette," I said. "My name ain't no Lala. It's Lafayette."

I turned away from both of them and stared out the window. If you ever had a brother who didn't *like* you, then I don't have to explain it. Feels like being a stranger in your own house, like *everything* that used to mean something doesn't anymore. Even your own name. Newcharlie'd hated my guts since Mama died, and he wasn't shy about letting anybody listening know it. Most times when he and Aaron got to talking, I just stayed quiet. If I was real quiet, it was like I was invisible. And if I was invisible, Newcharlie couldn't hate me.

"What about white boys?" Aaron asked.

"White boys?! What you *think* about white boys?"

"Don't know, Cha. That's why I'm here asking you. You act like you know everything about Dominicans and Ricans and brothers, I figure—"

" 'Course I know about *white boys*," Newcharlie said. "They not even worth mentioning. It's like if you have a totem pole of badness, right? You got the brothers at the top, then the Dominicans and the Puerto Ricans in gangs, then the Puerto Ricans not in gangs—and maybe some of those Chinese guys that's in gangs—"

"They know karate and stuff, too," Aaron said. "Like Jackie Chan. Jackie Chan can mess some brothers up, yo."

"Yeah, like if they know karate, then they probably go before the Puerto Ricans in gangs—"

"Except if the gangbangers got guns." Aaron looked over at me. "Blow somebody's head off."

I chewed on my bottom lip and didn't say anything. Once, before he went to Rahway, Charlie took me to see a Jackie Chan movie. When we came out of the movies, I started kicking and chopping and stuff, telling Charlie I wished I was Chinese so then I could know karate. Charlie put his hand on my shoulder and turned me toward him.

"Not all Chinese people know karate," he said. "That's a stereotype."

I didn't know what he was talking about, but his hand was hard on my shoulder, so I stopped chopping.

"Like when people say all black people are lazy or something," Charlie said.

I shrugged. A few months later I saw another movie. Only it wasn't Jackie Chan and it wasn't about karate. It was about this couple and they had this land-lord who lived upstairs who was supposed to be Chi-nese or something. Only he wasn't really. He was some guy making believe. When people in the audi-ence started laughing at the way the guy was talking, I felt weird, like it wasn't right.

"But if they know karate," Newcharlie was saying, "then they can kick a gun out of a gangbanger's hand, right?"

"Yeah," Aaron said. "You right. If they're fast enough. Don't a bullet travel at the speed of sound or something?"

"Depend on the gun, probably," Newcharlie said.

I wanted to remind Newcharlie about that day at the Jackie Chan flick, about his hand on my shoulder and what he'd said. And I wanted to tell Newcharlie that he had the totem pole idea all screwed up. If brothers were at the top, that meant they were the least bad. Anybody who knew even the tiniest bit about totem poles knew that the most important was at the bottom. But I bit my bottom lip and didn't say anything.

"Then after every every every body else," New-charlie was saying, "*then* you got white boys."

"What about that guy David?" Aaron asked. "The one from Rahway?"

I looked at Newcharlie in time to see him glance at me in the mirror, then cut his eyes back at Aaron. He wasn't allowed to talk about Rahway in front of me. Ty'ree didn't allow it. But Ty'ree was at work, and Newcharlie took every chance he could get to do the opposite of what Ty'ree said. He turned toward Aaron and leaned back against our dresser. Then he dropped his voice real low.

"I saw him make a knife out a slipper spoon," he said. "His moms had sent him one 'cause he kept say-ing his shoes was getting too small, and since she couldn't afford to buy him a new pair of shoes, she sent him some Vaseline and one of those things make putting your shoes on easier—I know they got an-other name, but he called it a slipper spoon." New-charlie eyed me, daring me to give the right name for it. I looked up at the ceiling and didn't say anything. I loved stories about Rahway.

"Every night I'd hear something scraping and scraping—real soft against the floor, like you had to listen real hard to hear. Sounded like a shy cat against a screen door—just like a little whisper of a scrape, but I knew what it was, so it sounded real loud to me. Like a clock ticking away somebody's life."

"How he gonna sharpen it on the floor, yo?"

Newcharlie rolled his eyes. "Floors in Rahway ain't regular floors. Everything there's made out of cement—walls, ceilings, floors—like you living inside a big gray rock. Winter you feel like you'll freeze to death inside that rock. Summer you think you gonna fry."

He stared into the mirror. Only he wasn't looking at himself anymore. He was looking somewhere else. Someplace far away.

"Everywhere, everywhere cement," he said, his voice dropping lower. "And all of us always marching in a line—to the bathroom, to grub hall, to yard time. No talking, just marching, marching. Say one word and the C.O.'s calling your last name and taking something away from you—no TV, no yard time, no rec hall. . . ." He was still looking at that faroff place, but he was whispering now. "No you. No more."

I pressed my back into the wall, the white white walls Mama had painted to make our room bright, and tried to imagine my brother inside that stone place.

The place he'd gone back to after Mama's funeral. No Mama. No name.

"Who that guy kill, Cha?" Aaron said.

Newcharlie blinked and looked from me to Aaron like he wasn't sure who we were or why we were there.

"Who?"

"That guy David, yo. The one with the slipper spoon," Aaron said. "What's wrong with you, man? You're like 'beam me up' or something."

"It's not deep, A. I'm just trying . . . to remember . . . all of it. Few days later David showed me the slipper spoon, only it wasn't a slipper spoon no more. He moved it real light across his finger and one drop of blood came out. Reddest blood I'd ever seen in my life. I mean, he like barely touched his finger and that drop of blood was there. His finger was real pale, and that blood just stood out on it. All thick and red. I looked at that blood and knew the next person come in contact with that slipper spoon was never gonna hear the words 'happy birthday' again."

"Who he kill?" Aaron asked again.

"Yeah," Newcharlie said. "I'd have to put David higher on the totem pole than other white boys."

Aaron grinned. "You ain't gonna say 'cause of Lala?"

Newcharlie nodded.

"I know he didn't kill anybody," I said. "I know the C.O. found that *shoehorn* under David's pillow one day while ya'll were out in the yard and David got sent off to another place—worse than Rahway."

Newcharlie gave me a dirty look. "That's what you think, stupid. That's what Ty'ree says to tell you, but that ain't what happened. And since you think you know so much, I'm *really* not gonna say. I almost said, too. Then you had to go and open your fat mouth. That's what you get, you little . . ." I waited for him to say it, but he didn't and I felt my stomach relax.

He turned back to the mirror. Newcharlie was wearing a plaid long-sleeved shirt and baggy jeans. He unbuttoned the top button, then buttoned it again and checked himself out one more time.

"You ready?" Newcharlie asked.

Aaron nodded.

"Then let's step." He looked at me. "When Ty'ree gets home, you tell him we just left too, you hear me?"

I kept staring out the window.

"Your brother talking to you, man." Aaron said.

"Yeah—I hear you."

"Later, Milagros killer."

"Oh shoot." Aaron laughed. "That's cold, man."

"It's true," Charlie said.

I swallowed and looked down at my hands so Newcharlie wouldn't see my eyes tearing up. I could hear the door slamming in the living room and him and Aaron running down the stairs, taking them two at a time the way they always did. A few minutes later I heard Newcharlie calling out to somebody. It was gray out. I stared at the sky and tried not to let his words sink in. I stared until the window blurred.

"I didn't kill her," I whispered.

Then I lay back on my bed and prayed it would pour down rain.

TWO

OUR DADDY HAD BEEN A HERO. WHEN MAMA was still pregnant with me, our daddy was sitting in Central Park reading the paper. It was wintertime, but he liked to go over to the park and sit. He liked the quiet and the cold together. He liked the sound his newspaper made when he turned the pages in the wind. Ty'ree says this woman had been jogging around the lake near where Daddy was. She was jogging with her dog when the dog decided to take off after a bird. The lake was frozen, so I guess the dog just figured it could run straight across. But right in the middle the ice started cracking away, and the dog went under. Daddy looked up to see the screaming lady running after the dog—saw the dog way out, bobbing in and out of the water. Ty'ree says Daddy pulled the lady out first, then the dog. The dog and the lady lived, but my daddy died of hypothermia.

"He went out stupid," Newcharlie always says now. "Saving a dog and a white woman is a stupid way to die. Only thing in the world you need to save is your own self."

"You used to want to save stray animals," I remind Newcharlie. "You used to pray to St. Francis."

How do I do it, Cha? I'd asked that first night a long time ago, the night he told me about St. Francis.

Charlie sat up in his bed and put his hands together under his chin. *Like this.* "*Dear Lord and St. Francis of Assisi. Me and my brother know you both love animals as much as we do. We know how you saved that dog that was drowning in Central Park. You sent our daddy in there. We're not mad about it or anything. Not anymore. We don't have another daddy, but there's a lot of other animals need saving. So please don't let none get killed by starving or freezing to* death in the cold. *Don't let none get hit by cars or beat up by stupid kids. Just let them all have food and someplace warm. And if you could, could you please give dogs nine lives the same as cats?"*

And turtles too, I added. *Please.*

Turtles too, Charlie said. *Amen.*

Amen, I whispered.

Charlie unclasped his hands and lay back on the bed. *Now watch,* he said. *When you dream, it's gonna be full of happy animals.*

He was right.

But that was a long long time ago. Back when we were a family. Back before Rahway and Mama dying. Back before . . . before Charlie became somebody else.

"I never cared about no dogs," Newcharlie says. But he doesn't look at me when he says it, because he knows I know he's lying.

All we got now is one other brother—Ty'ree. Ty'ree's just the opposite of Newcharlie. He'll tell you in a minute he's got a soft spot for me and don't care what people say about it. Newcharlie would never call me Lala in front of Ty'ree. He just knows better. People who knew Mama say if Ty'ree was a woman, he'd be her twin, even though two people made him, he's all Milagros' child. Milagros was my mama. Her name

18

means "miracle" in Spanish, and maybe it was a miracle that she had a demon-seed son like Newcharlie.

Mama was born in Bayamón—that's in Puerto Rico—but her family came here when she was real little. I can only speak a little bit of Spanish, because Mama used to say it was better if we learned good English. But I'm taking Spanish now. Figure if I learn to speak Mama's language, I'll have a little bit more of her to hold on to.

My great-aunt Cecile's all the time saying dead don't have to mean dead and gone, and I like to believe that. I got two scratched-up pictures of Mama left. One of the pictures is of me and her outside on the stoop. Mama's sitting and I'm standing bending over her to show her something I got in my hand. Mama's wearing a light-blue dress and she has her hair out so that it's all curly around her shoulders. In the picture she's smiling at the thing I'm showing her like she's real proud. I look real close at that picture all the time, but I still can't remember what it was I was showing her. The other picture's of me and Charlie and Mama. We're all dressed up and smiling. Maybe it was Easter. Mama has her arms around me and Charlie's shoulders. We both look a little bit like her in that picture, but I'm much darker—like Mama said my daddy was.

There used to be a lot of other pictures but they got burned. Newcharlie had a fit one Saturday and burned them all, but we're not allowed to talk about it.

Sometimes I wonder what happened to that lady and that dog my daddy saved. There's always stories about people getting saved and then giving the people who saved them money or people coming along years later and naming their kids after the people, but none of that ever happened to us. My daddy's name was Lafayette too, and I wonder if there's a little white kid somewhere named after him. Maybe the lady is still jogging around Central Park. Maybe she keeps her dog on a leash now though. And maybe once in a while she sees in her head my daddy running toward her on a half frozen lake. Or maybe she didn't have any kids and doesn't remember my daddy at all.

THREE

After Newcharlie and Aaron left, I went into the living room and turned on the television. On Friday nights Ty'ree let me watch it as much as I wanted as long as I took one weekend day for homework. I usually chose Sunday—usually starting in the late late afternoon or the minute Ty'ree started getting after me—whichever came first.

I flipped through the channels for a while, then sat back against the couch and watched music videos. I couldn't really tell one from the other. Most of them had some guy standing there rapping and a lot of pretty girls dancing around him. Or the guy was driving a fancy car with pretty girls in it. Once in a while the guy would be in a swimming pool with pretty girls. That was the one on now—a guy with a lot of rings on his fingers rapping to some pretty girls in bikinis.

Newcharlie liked listening to music and said he was gonna be a rapper. Aaron said he was gonna be one, too. Either that or a car salesman. I guess he figured he'd sell cars to rappers who would fill them with pretty girls. Thing about rapping though, Newcharlie said, is you gotta do it now. Most rappers weren't much older than him. Sometimes he and Aaron sat in our room all day long, making up rhymes and slapping each other five when something came off sounding right. But I hadn't seen them taking any real steps— like making some tapes and calling up a radio station to ask for a few minutes on the air.

I turned the volume down low. The apartment felt big and quiet with nobody in it. It's not that big—just four rooms: me and Newcharlie's room, then Ty'ree's room right next to us. His room used to be Mama's. Then there's a long hallway leading to one big room that's both the living room and the dining room. If you go right, there's a dining-room table and chairs. If you go left, there's the couch and stuff. The door to come in and out is between the couch and dining-room table. You walk through the living-room side to get to the kitchen. You have to walk through the kitchen to get to the bathroom.

Newcharlie had put plants in all the windows—spider plants and ferns and some other ones I don't know the name of. He'd learned a lot about plants at Rahway. It was strange to see him messing around them on Saturday mornings, taking off the dead leaves and giving them water. Sometimes he put these little sticks of plant food in the dirt. Once I even caught him *talking* to them, telling this sickly-looking fern that it better toughen up if it wanted to make it in the world.

The sun had come out again, and I watched it bounce off the plants and sprinkle itself over the dining-room table. When I closed my eyes to just a sliver, I could see Mama sitting at that table, playing with her eyebrow the way she did when she was worrying, her hair coming loose from its braid. I watched my ghost mama for a while. She looked peaceful sitting there even if she was worrying.

"Hey, Mama," I whispered. "Can you make some chicken for dinner tonight?"

Mama looked over at me and smiled, a quiet, far-away smile. I blinked and she wasn't there anymore.

I got a thousand dollars in my pocket, the guy in the rap video was saying. I leaned back against the sofa and watched him do a sort of swim-dance around the girls.

After a while, I heard Ty'ree coming up the stairs. He always whistled the same song—a song our mama used to sing to us called "Me and Bobby McGee" about a woman hitchhiking with her boyfriend in Louisiana and how free she felt whenever she played her harmonica. When Ty'ree sang the words sometimes, it made me want to get a harmonica and get out onto the road. Maybe see a sunset. Once Ty'ree took me to Central Park and we watched the sun go down over the lake my daddy got hypothermia in. It was real pretty. Pretty and sad. Most times, though, it just sets and then it's night and what you notice is the day and the night—not the sunset in between. On the highway you probably get all four parts—the sunrise, the day, the sunset, and the night.

"Yo!" Ty'ree yelled.

"Yo back," I said, holding up my hand without turning my head. I felt Ty'ree slap it and smiled.

"Where's your brother?"

I shrugged.

Ty'ree sat down on the couch beside me. He was tall and skinny-looking but not really. When he wasn't wearing a shirt, you could see all his muscles. But with his clothes on he looked skinny. He used to have locks, but he cut them off when he started working full-time, and now his hair is short and neat like an old man's even though he's only twenty-two. He leaned back against the couch and loosened his tie. I guess Ty'ree's like our daddy. He works and pays the rent and buys groceries and stuff. After Mama died, the people at the publishing house let him start working full-time. Now he's the mailroom manager there and says the work isn't so bad, but once in a while people blame you for stuff that isn't your fault. Ty'ree says it's not even worth getting mad about really. He says that's how it is in the whole world, people always looking for someone else to blame, so he might as well get used to it.

"Where's your brother, Laf?" he asked again.

"Just left."

Ty'ree looked at me, a slow smile coming to his face. He had the best smile in the world. Everybody said so. When he smiled, it made me think about when I used to go to church, how I'd sit there staring at this stained-glass window of Jesus with all the kids around him. Jesus was smiling and the kids were smiling and everything seemed peaceful and right. That's what Ty'ree's smile was like. Peaceful and right. Once I heard Mrs. Williams who lives downstairs call him St. Ty'ree, and I heard Ty'ree laugh and say, *But I ain't dead yet, Mrs. W.*

"That what he said to tell me?" Ty'ree raised his eyebrows at me.

I shook my head and glued my eyes to the TV.

"Yeah, right!" Ty'ree rubbed my head and I smiled, taking a swing at his hand and missing.

"He really did just leave, T—like maybe a half hour ago."

"He say where he was going?"

"Nah."

Ty'ree frowned. "Boy better not be out there getting in any more trouble, that's for sure. And you better not be getting into any trouble either." He tapped the back of my neck.

If Newcharlie got into trouble again, they'd send him off to someplace worse than Rahway. The social worker said that she'd also have to send me either down south with Aunt Cecile or into foster care, 'cause if Newcharlie got into trouble again, it meant Ty'ree couldn't handle us.

"You hear me, Laf?"

"Do I *look* like I'm getting into trouble, man?!"

"Looks can be deceiving, li'l brother."

"Well, I'm not. I'm not Newcharlie and I'm not getting into trouble. Just sitting here watching some TV, that's all. A little TV never hurt nobody."

Ty'ree looked at me for a moment, then smiled again.

"Well it *didn't*. Not like watching a video's going to teach me how to hold up a candy store."

"Hey, we don't need to talk about that, all right?"

I nodded. Our house was full of stuff we didn't need to talk about.

"How come you ain't outside, Laf?"

"First you tell me don't be getting into trouble, then—"

"Little outside never hurt nobody," Ty'ree said, mimicking me.

I tried not to laugh but couldn't help it. Ty'ree could always make me laugh.

"PJ and Smitty visiting their cousin this weekend," I said.

"Out in Brooklyn?"

I nodded. Me and Smitty had been friends forever, been in the same class since third grade. Him and his little brother, PJ, lived right down the block, and we all hung out once in a while. But sometimes Smitty'd get to asking questions about Mama dying—stuff I didn't care to talk about.

"Can you make chicken for dinner, Ty?"

He jutted his chin toward the kitchen. "I read your mind. Took it out the freezer before I went to work this morning."

"You gonna fry it?"

"Yeah."

We sat watching TV for a while. Ty'ree wasn't really watching though. He looked like he was thinking deep about things.

"You thinking about Mama?" I asked.

Ty'ree shrugged. "Not really. Kind of, I guess. Why do you ask?"

" 'Cause I'm always thinking about her."

"Me too."

Me and Ty'ree stared at the TV, feeling Mama somewhere nearby, and the house and my head chockfull with things we weren't allowed to talk about.

FOUR

NOBODY KNOWS WHERE CHARLIE GOT THE GUN
he used to hold up Poncho's candy store three years
ago. Not even Ty'ree. When the cops showed up at our
house that night, Mama and Ty'ree were sitting at the
dining-room table. Ty'ree had just cashed his check
from the publishing company where he worked part-
time, and Mama was filling out a money order for the
rent. Ever since I can remember, Ty'ree had sat with
Mama at the table, the dim light from the floor lamp
in the corner turning them both a soft golden brown.
While Mama filled out the money order and figured

out how to pay some of the other bills, Ty'ree made grocery lists and school supply lists and added and re-added the cost of everything. Some evenings he'd sit clipping coupons for the cereals we liked and the laundry detergent Mama used. He'd put these in an envelope on top of the refrigerator and take them down when he and Mama sat at the table, figuring and re-figuring.

That's what they were doing the night the cops knocked on our door looking for Charlie.

I was sitting in front of the television watching the news, because on weeknights Mama'd let us watch only one hour of regular television and then as much news as we wanted. I didn't really care for watching the news, but it was better than nothing.

Charlie had told Mama he was going to an after-school program to get help with his math homework. When he came in at seven that night, the news was going off and me, Mama, Ty'ree, and the cops were all waiting. Charlie had been too dumb to get rid of the gun. The cops found it and two hundred and fifty dollars in his pockets. Charlie was twelve and a half. Too young for real jail. So they sent him to Rahway Home for Boys.

It was one of the few times I'd ever seen Mama cry.

I turned and eyed Ty'ree now. He was leaning against the back of the couch with his eyes closed. I turned the TV down a bit more. I had been twelve for only three weeks but it felt like forever. Every day Ty'ree found a way to remind me not to end up like Newcharlie. But I wasn't Newcharlie. I was Lafayette. I had a bit more sense in my head.

I could hear kids running up and down outside in the street and some girls playing jump rope. I heard a fire truck go by and a little kid crying for his mama. We live on the sixth floor. If you hang out our window and look way over to the left, you can see Central Park, the very edge of it near the ice-skating rink. You can see the tops of the trees—they were turning all different colors now. And you can see lots of cars. If you look to your right, you can see the George Washington Bridge. Early in the morning you can hear the traffic coming over it. Right across the street is a bunch more buildings like ours—old gray-and-beige buildings with lots of floors and lots of apartments. Years and years and years ago the buildings used to be fancy, Ty'ree says. But not anymore. Now they're just buildings filled with people getting by. That's what me and Ty'ree and Newcharlie were—people getting by.

"Ty'ree," I whispered. "You asleep?"

Ty'ree shook his head.

I looked down at the remote control, then back up at the television.

"W's up?"

"Can you tell me something?"

"Maybe," Ty'ree said sleepily. "If I know it."

I tried not to think about Newcharlie's face when he said the words, when he called me Milagros killer.

"Can you tell me about when . . . when Mama died?"

Ty'ree frowned, then slowly opened his eyes. "It's Friday night, Lafayette. Go play some ball."

I shrugged. "Don't feel like it."

"It's gonna be winter soon—then it'll be too cold to be hanging."

"Said I don't *feel* like it."

"What do you want to know about it?" Ty'ree asked. He sounded tired. After a moment he put his hand on my knee. I wanted to put my hand over his but didn't.

"Just . . . like . . . like how come?"

"You know how come. She had diabetes. She went into a insulin shock."

"But . . . *why?*"

" 'Cause she had too much insulin in her. Her body just—just sort of shut down."

I bit my bottom lip. "Then what happened?"

Ty'ree sighed and leaned back against the couch. "You found her the next morning," he said. He sounded real patient, like he was talking to a very little kid. "She hadn't got up to fix your breakfast. You were in the fourth grade. You always liked oatmeal in the morning. You tried to wake her up to fix you some."

"Where were you, T?"

"I'd left for school already. I'd just graduated the day before, and I was going to pick up my diploma and say good-bye to people."

"And Newcharlie was at Rahway, right?"

Ty'ree nodded. "He'd been there for two months when Mom died."

Once Mama had said to me that time is like a movie—something you watch real close wanting to catch every line, every action, every moment. Then it passes and you feel like no time passed at all. She said that when her parents died, time didn't stop the way people always say it does. She said it just became more *precise*—every minute, hour, day mattered that much

33

more. Charlie had been in Rahway for two months. There were four days between the time I found her and the day we buried her. The morning I found Mama, the clock beside her bed said 7:44. *Mama*, I'd whispered. *You're oversleeping.* And now years have gone by—like no time at all.

"You remember the last thing you said to Mama, T?"

Ty'ree smiled. "I told her to make sure that when she ironed my green shirt, she didn't put any startch in it. I didn't like starch in that shirt for some reason."

"You like starch in the other ones, though."

"Yeah, I do."

I twirled the remote around in my hands. "I think I told her she was oversleeping," I said. "But she didn't hear me. Her hair was hanging down over her face. I moved her hair away but I didn't call nobody. I should've called somebody."

"You did," Ty'ree said.

"But that was later on. It was too late then."

"It was too late when you found her, Laf."

I put the TV on mute and watched some people dance across the screen. They looked so happy dancing, like dancing was the best thing in the world.

"I was wearing my Brooklyn shirt," I whispered.

"And jeans. Mama was wearing her yellow pajamas, the ones with toasters on them. Remember those?"

Ty'ree nodded but didn't say anything.

"Me and Charlie had given her those pajamas for Christmas the year before. They'd been on sale, and me and Charlie couldn't believe we had enough money to buy Mama pajamas. With *toasters* on them. She always always always burned the toast."

"She thought we liked it that way." Ty'ree looked down at his hands and smiled.

"But how come?"

" 'Cause none of us ever had the heart to tell her we didn't."

I swallowed and stared at the TV. "Because we loved her too much to hurt her feelings."

We didn't say anything for a long time. It was starting to get dark out. When I looked over at Ty'ree, he was frowning down at the floor.

He bent over and picked up a straw wrapper. "I told Charlie to sweep. You see him sweeping?"

I shrugged. "He could have done it while I was at school or something."

"He *didn't* sweep," Ty'ree said, his voice getting loud. "Look at this floor! Look at it."

It looked fine to me. "I'll sweep it."

"No, *I'll* sweep it," he said, and got up and went into the kitchen. "I have to do everything in this house. Everything." I could hear him in there banging around. Then I heard him sniff and blow his nose. A few minutes later I could hear him making choking sounds. I went into my room then and closed the door, not wanting to hear Ty'ree crying, not wanting to hear anything. A long time ago he had given me his green shirt. I pulled it out of my drawer and spread it across my pillow, then put my face in it.

"Mama," I whispered, "wake up."

FIVE

AFTER MAMA DIED, MY GREAT-AUNT CECILE
came up from South Carolina saying she was going to
take me and Ty'ree back home to live with her. She's a
small woman with white hair, tiny silver glasses, and
hands that shake whenever she eats or drinks something. The two things I noticed right off were how she
smelled like the candy part of candy apples and how
perfect her teeth were. Ty'ree said it would be two
thousand miracles rolled into one if they were real.

I had met Aunt Cecile only once, when I was real
small and Mama had taken us all down south for our

daddy's uncle's funeral. Aunt Cecile was our daddy's aunt. I didn't remember much about that time, but Aunt Cecile remembered me.

"You were just an ant of a thing," she said, picking me up like I was still two instead of nine and squeezing me to her. "And look at you now, just as beautiful as I don't know what."

I'd never been called beautiful by anybody, and after Aunt Cecile said that, I went into the bathroom and checked myself in the mirror. Ty'ree always said I looked like our daddy. He was dark and curly-headed with brown eyes. My eyes are more black than brown, and my hair's more kinky than curly. Ty'ree makes me keep it cut short, sort of a fade. And when it's real short, you can see where it starts out as curls. I looked at myself in the mirror and tried to smile like Ty'ree, but one of my front teeth overlaps the other in a way that makes me look a little bit meaner than I actually am. Still, maybe Aunt Cecile was right. Maybe I was beautiful underneath it all.

ALL DAY LONG, PEOPLE HAD BEEN COMING IN and out of our apartment, bringing us food and juice and talking about how sorry they were and how big I was getting. Someone even brought by a pound of bacon, two cans of Spam, a dozen eggs, and a loaf of Wonder bread in case we got up in the morning and didn't want to eat the other stuff. Ty'ree and Aunt Cecile took everything everybody brought us and thanked them. I sat in the living room mostly, staring at the television set and wishing everybody would just leave us alone. I wanted Mama to come home. Wanted to hear her coming up those stairs singing that "Me and Bobby McGee" song the way she always did.

Me and Ty'ree were both wearing black suits. Mine was too short at the wrists 'cause Mama had bought it the year before for me to wear on special occasions like school assembly and church. Since there hadn't been that many assemblies and I usually wore pants with a shirt and a tie to church, the suit had hung in my closet until Ty'ree pulled it out the day before Mama's funeral.

They had let Charlie come to the funeral and stay with us for a few hours afterward. When Aunt Cecile saw him with those two guards from Rahway, she crossed herself and pressed her handkerchief against her mouth. Charlie stood real stiff while she hugged him, his eyes sweeping over everybody, checking us all out. There wasn't any feeling in them. Just hard, flat eyes that didn't belong to the Charlie they had taken away.

"Charlie," I whispered, trying to hold his hand, "Mama *died*."

Charlie snatched his hand away from mine and glared at me. "How come you ain't save her, huh?" he said. "If I was here, I would've saved her."

I stared at the guy standing in front of me. It wasn't Charlie. Charlie would never talk that way—never blame me for anything. This was somebody different. New. Newcharlie.

"I *tried*," I whispered, taking tiny breaths to keep from crying.

"I would've saved her." Newcharlie turned away from me, went over to the corner, and crouched down against the wall. He stayed that way, glaring at his hands.

The two guards watched him the whole time. By the time he had to go, I was relieved. *I didn't kill her,* I kept wanting to say to Newcharlie, but I couldn't. And on the way out of the house, when Newcharlie looked back at me and Ty'ree, then punched the wall, I felt like he was punching *me.* Ty'ree had his arm around me, and when Newcharlie punched the wall, he pulled me closer. We stood there listening and could hear Newcharlie crying all the way down the stairs.

"Charlie," I whispered. Because he sounded like I remembered, like he did when that dog died. Hurt and small and lonely. "Charlie, don't cry. Please don't cry." His crying sounds kept coming though, but they got softer and softer, moving farther and farther away from us.

"Charlie," I whispered, burying my head into Ty'ree's arm. "Where'd you go, man? Where'd you go?"

SIX

THAT NIGHT, THE NIGHT OF THE DAY WE BURIED
Mama, Aunt Cecile sat down in Mama's chair at the
table and told me and Ty'ree about her plan to move us
back home with her.

"We're already at home," I remember saying.

Aunt Cecile smiled her perfect-teeth smile and
shook her head. "You're just two boys," she said.
"And Charlie won't be home for at least another two
years. When he gets out, he can come on down south
too."

"You want to go live down south, Lafayette?" Ty'ree called to me.

I shook my head.

Ty'ree raised his hands and gave Aunt Cecile his St. Ty'ree smile. "Guess we'll be staying here then."

He and Aunt Cecile went back and forth for a long time, Aunt Cecile saying Ty'ree was too young to try to raise me and Ty'ree telling her of his plans to work full-time now that he'd graduated high school.

While they talked, I felt Mama sit down beside me and I laid my head against her shoulder. It was warm and soft and smelled like the honeysuckle oil she liked to put in her hair. But when I looked a few minutes later, it was just an orange pillow underneath my face, the pillow Mama had sewed back up after I had picked a hole in it.

After a while Aunt Cecile went into the kitchen and asked if me and Ty'ree wanted something to eat. We both said yes, and she fixed us each a big plate of food. I ate mine in front of the television halfway listening to Ty'ree and Aunt Cecile talk about how me and Ty'ree would and wouldn't get by living on our own.

Ty'ree had been accepted at MIT. I knew that was good, 'cause people made all kinds of fusses about the school and about Ty'ree at his graduation. Every time we turned around, he was going up onstage to get another award. He was good in science and stuff. Sometimes he'd take me to the park with him, and I'd get to watch him and his friends launch rockets they'd built. For a long time he'd talked about wanting to work with NASA. After Mama died, he changed his mind about everything. Even stopped going to the park to launch rockets with his friends. Most of the guys he hung with went away to college. Ty'ree had gone to a special high school for smart kids. He was the only guy in our neighborhood to get in. Before Mama died, some guys used to make fun of him and call him Professor. But later on, once he started working full-time and taking care of me, people started showing him respect, saying, "W's up, Ty," when he came home in the evening. Slapping him five and asking after me and Newcharlie. Ty'ree said he didn't really care about not going to college, that keeping his little bit of family together was the most important thing. But once in a while he'd go over and visit some of his old homeboys who were home for Thanksgiving break or Christmas vacation. When he came home those nights, he didn't have much to say, just sat at the dining-room table slowly going through the pages of his high school yearbook, looking lost. Looking like he'd left something big behind him.

Aunt Cecile stayed with us for two weeks. By the time she left, all of Mama's stuff was gone and Mama's room had become Ty'ree's.

"At least you won't have to fuss about me sleeping on the couch during your Saturday-morning cartoons," Ty'ree had said when he caught me standing in Mama's room looking around for her things.

"I liked you better on the couch," I said. "I liked it better when Mama was sleeping in here. Where's her stuff?"

"Took it down to Goodwill this morning."

I opened the closet door. Ty'ree's basketball sneakers were on the floor where Mama's green sandals used to be. His shirts were hanging where Mama's dresses used to hang. Her black winter coat and yellow wool scarf were gone. I sniffed the closet. It still smelled like her.

"If I had a bad dream, Mama'd let me come sleep with her."

"You can come sleep with me now if you have a bad dream," Ty'ree said.

"It ain't the same, T."

"Do you remember the time she—"

I closed the closet door and looked at Ty'ree, waiting for him to finish. But he just shook his head. The *whole* room still smelled like Mama, like coffee and perfume and . . . It smelled like the way she laughed. Tinkly. It smelled like the memories of her—like how she used to try to hold my hand when we crossed the street. Even when I was nine, she was still trying to hold my hand. And I'd snatch it away from her and frown. Then she'd laugh and pull me to her. Sometimes I let her do that—walk across the street with her arm around my shoulder while men whistled at her and asked if I was her boyfriend. She was real pretty, my mama was. And some Friday nights she'd put on music and me and her would dance and dance. . . .

Me and Ty'ree hadn't cried yet. At the funeral we'd sat up front and let everyone give us hugs and pats on the backs and sorry looks without even flinching. But that day, after we'd put Aunt Cecile on a bus heading back down south, we stood in Mama's room that was now Ty'ree's watching the sun coming in through the window. Ty'ree had left up the flowered curtains Mama'd bought downtown, and for some reason this was sadder than anything to me. It seemed wrong—a big, blue-plaid boy comforter on the bed and Mama's lady curtains at the window. I went over and rubbed the curtains against my face.

"This is all, huh, T?" I whispered. "This is all we got left of Mama."

Ty'ree shook his head. "Nah, Lafayette," he said. "That ain't all."

I didn't know what he meant but I couldn't ask. My throat was starting to fill up with all the days Mama had been dead and me not crying. All the tears were jamming themselves together and pushing their way out.

Ty'ree came over to me and looked at my face for a minute. Then, without saying anything else, he pulled me to him and we stood there crying until the sun was gone.

SEVEN

I HAD FALLEN ASLEEP ON TY'REE'S SHIRT AND woke to the smell of chicken frying and Ty'ree singing "Me and Bobby McGee" in the kitchen. I could hear him moving around, lifting the covers on pots and getting things out of the refrigerator. I rolled onto my back and thought about the dream I'd just had. Ty'ree and Aunt Cecile had agreed that I'd spend every summer down south with her, and when Newcharlie came home, he'd spend summers there too. The first summer I went, Aunt Cecile had pointed me down a path that led to a stream chock-full of rainbow trout. I had been dreaming about that stream, about trout jumping up onto the fishing pole Aunt Cecile had given me. In the dream the fish wiggled and wiggled, their rainbow scales flickering in the sun. I pulled a fish off my line and let it dance its last dance against the bank, then put it in a pail half filled with water. I was carrying the fish back to Aunt Cecile, and she was going to fry it up. Then a shadow came over the path, and when I looked up, I saw Newcharlie standing there frowning down at me. He knocked the pail out of my hand and the fish lay on the ground between us, its eyes wide and glassy. When I opened my mouth to say something to him, no words came out, and me and Newcharlie just stood there. That's when I woke up.

It was dark out now, and a steady rain was pinging against the window. I wondered where Newcharlie was, wondered if he'd gotten home yet. I closed my eyes and tried to remember more stuff about what it was like before he went to Rahway. Sometimes me and him would sit out on the stoop waiting for Mama to come home and he'd tell me about girls who liked him and guys who thought they were bad. Sometimes me and him would get to laughing so hard about something that we couldn't stop. I remember this one day we were laughing like that and Aaron came up to the stoop and asked what we were laughing at. Me and Charlie just looked at each other and busted out laughing even harder. I don't think we even answered Aaron. We probably didn't even have an answer. And sometimes Newcharlie walked down the block with his arm around my shoulder bragging to everybody about how smart I was.

Him and my big brother's gonna be rocket scientists, he'd say. *Better watch out, or else I'll get them to send your butt to the moon!*

"Mama," I whispered. "Make them send the old Charlie home."

Ty'ree stuck his head in the door. Bright light from the hall came in with him.

"Yo, yo, yo," he said. "Time to get up and eat, sleepyhead."

"What time's it?"

"Little bit after seven. You feel like going to the movies tonight after we eat?"

I sat up, rubbed my eyes, and nodded. "See what?"

Ty'ree shrugged. "I don't know. Figured we'd go downtown to the Quad and see what's playing."

"I don't want to see no art movie. You always want

to take me to see those boring old art movies. Half the time I don't even know what they're about."

Ty'ree shook his head and smiled. "You'll figure it out someday."

"I don't want to figure it out *someday*. I want to see a movie I can figure out while I'm *watching* it. Only reason you asking me is 'cause nobody else'll go with you."

"Only reason I'm taking you to the Quad is 'cause I'm not gonna spend eight fifty on some karate movie or action feature about some outer-space somebody wanting to blow up the Earth."

I grinned. "It could happen, you know. We don't really know about life on other planets."

"And we ain't gonna find out about it tonight. Come on and wash up. I got food almost on the table."

He disappeared out the door, and I got up and went to the bathroom.

Going to the art movies with Ty'ree wasn't really *that* bad. If we saw something that was way deep, he'd always figure out a way to break it down for me.

Ty'ree had fried chicken and made mashed potatoes and corn with red peppers in it. He'd fixed me and him a plate and put two slices of bread on mine because I eat bread with everything.

51

I sat down at the dining-room table. "We got any soda, T?"

"Ginger ale," Ty'ree called from the kitchen. "You want some?"

I frowned, not even knowing why I asked. It was the only kind of soda Ty'ree bought when he went shopping. If I had some extra money, I'd pick up a big bottle of orange or grape soda. I hadn't had extra money in a while.

"Nah. Just water, please."

Ty'ree came out with two big glasses of ice water and sat down across from me. We ate for a while without saying anything. Ty'ree'd learned to cook from Mama and from reading cookbooks. There were always two or three cookbooks in the bathroom, because he usually read them in there the way most people read the sports section or magazines.

"You say grace?" he asked me.

I closed my eyes. "Thank you, oh Lord and Ty'ree, for getting me something good to eat before I starved to death dreaming of fish. Amen."

When I opened my eyes, Ty'ree was smiling. I smiled back.

"You really dreamed about fish?"

I nodded.

"Aunt Cecile would tell us to play a number," Ty'ree said. "Fish is supposed to mean something. I remember her talking to somebody about it, saying she'd dreamed about fish one night and played whatever number it was and then two days later she hit for like three hundred dollars."

"What number was it?"

Ty'ree shrugged. "Even if I knew, we wouldn't play. Figure if Aunt Cecile hit for three hundred, she must have lost about six hundred—as much as she plays and as little as she hits." Ty'ree picked up his chicken wing, took a bite, and chewed slowly.

"In the dream Newcharlie came along and knocked the bucket of fish outa my hand," I said. "You figure they got a number for brothers knocking fish outa your hand?"

Ty'ree didn't say anything for a minute. He was holding the chicken wing in his hand and had a far-away look about him. I was sorry I had even mentioned it. It was only a stupid dream anyway.

"You know I don't like you calling him that, Laf."

"He calls me worse. And that's who he is anyway. That ain't the same brother left this house that night."

"None of us are."

"But we didn't get *evil*." I stirred my potatoes around on my plate, not wanting to look at him.

"You got quiet," Ty'ree said. "You don't hardly leave the house."

"I hang with Smitty and PJ sometimes and sit on the stoop—"

"You used to *play*, Laf."

"Well, I was a little kid then."

Ty'ree shook his head. "You used to laugh all the time and make jokes and play freeze tag and handball. You used to always have something new to tell me or show me. You used to go to Poncho's and come back with potato chips and soda and go across the street to talk to people."

"Poncho don't want us in there after Charlie robbed him."

Ty'ree looked at me. "You know that's not true."

I stared at my plate. After Newcharlie got home, we all went around the corner to Poncho's and Charlie apologized. Poncho said he didn't hold any bad feelings 'cause Charlie had done his time. *I loved your mother*, Poncho said. *You're welcome here. All of you.*

"I don't like candy and stuff anymore anyway," I said.

"Yes you do, Laf. Don't lie. And what about the other stuff? What about how you used to come home and talk about everything you did and saw—"

"I was just a little kid! Little kids do that stuff."

"Nah," Ty'ree said. "That's not why."

I didn't say anything. Ty'ree thought he knew it all, but he didn't. He didn't know *anything*.

"You changed too!"

"I know. I stuck my head into my job, raising you and Charlie. And Charlie, I don't know. He went somewhere inside himself. You see it. See the way he sits there staring off sometimes."

I nodded, remembering all the times I woke to find Newcharlie sitting on the edge of his bed, with his hands hanging down between his knees, just staring out the window. "What's he thinking about anyway? When he stares like that?"

Ty'ree shook his head. "Maybe Rahway. Maybe Mama. Maybe me and you."

"He's not thinking about me. At least nothing I'd want to get inside his head and hear."

"He say where he was going?" Ty'ree asked.

"Uh-uh."

"He didn't say what time he'd be back either, did he?"

"Nah."

"You rather I put you in my room and share your room with Charlie?"

I looked up at Ty'ree trying to see if he was mad or serious. His face was calm, like he just wanted everything to be over with already.

"Nah. It ain't so bad no more. He don't speak to me is all."

"How come you don't just ignore him? Make like he's not even there."

" 'Cause he wasn't here for years!" I hadn't meant to yell. " 'Cause," I said, almost whispering. " 'Cause I want Charlie back. I want my brother. I want him to see me. And I want him not to think I . . . I was the reason Mama died. I *wasn't* the reason."

Ty'ree frowned and stopped eating. "He still saying that? I told that boy I'd—"

"No," I lied. "He don't say it anymore. But I know he still thinks it."

"Look, Lafayette." Ty'ree rubbed his hand over his head and sighed. "You weren't the reason. Mama had—"

"I should have called somebody! I should have tried to get her breathing again. I just sat there calling to her. Just sat there waiting for her to wake up. And

Newcharlie knows it. He knows I got scared and froze up."

"She was gone before you got there, Lafayette. I don't know what's gonna make you hear that it wasn't your fault."

"Charlie would've known what to do. Like that time with that dog that got hit by the car. He found some cardboard and put the dog on it, real careful 'cause he said the dog might have some broken bones. Then he got me to help him lift the dog over to the sidewalk. He made me call the animal emergency people. I wanted to stay there, but he made me go, told me to run." I looked up at Ty'ree. "By the time I got back, Charlie was holding the dog's head on his lap. The animal emergency people said that was the right thing to do. And then that stupid dog had to go and die anyway."

Ty'ree nodded. Every day Charlie would call the ASPCA to see if that dog was still living. And every night he'd ask Mama if we could adopt it. Mama said no 'cause me and her had allergies, and even if we didn't, our building didn't allow pets. Then one day the ASPCA told Charlie that the dog hadn't made it. That's what the guy said, *The dog didn't make it*, like the dog was on its way someplace or meeting somebody for lunch. "Didn't make it" is a stupid way to say something died. Charlie stayed in our room all afternoon. When he came out that night, Mama asked him how he was feeling.

Like nothing, Charlie said. *I don't feel like nothing anymore.*

Now Ty'ree looked at me, waiting for me to say something. I shrugged and stared down at my plate. Mama had been warm that morning. Warm like a person sleeping. Warm like that dog still was when we lifted it over to the curb. And when the stupid doctor told us Mama didn't make it, I felt like nothing, too. Like I could just dry up and disappear.

"I know I told you this a lot of times," Ty'ree said. "And I know other people have said it, too. But I'm gonna keep saying it, 'cause I know you need to keep hearing it. There wasn't anything you could have done, Lafayette."

"Miss Roberts from down the hall came first," I whispered. "I was screaming and she came and banged on the door. I was still screaming, but I got up to let her in."

Ty'ree didn't say anything, so I went on.

"She tried to blow in Mama's mouth. She told me

to call 911. I was crying. I couldn't go at first. I wanted to stay there with Mama."

"But then you went," Ty'ree said.

I looked up at him. "It took them a real long time to come."

"But you called them and they came, Laf. You called them and they came."

Me and Ty'ree sat there staring at our plates. I wasn't hungry anymore. I wanted to be out of the house suddenly, away from that day. I wanted to be in a dark theater somewhere, far away from our apartment. Far away from those men carrying Mama down the stairs while Miss Roberts held me and cried.

"Can we go to the movies now, T?"

Ty'ree nodded. "You want to see a blow-up-the-world movie?"

I shook my head. "Nah. Not really. I don't care if I have to think real hard. No subtitles though. Can stay home to *read*."

I looked up at Ty'ree and he smiled. I tried to smile back, but my lips felt quivery, so I got up and took our plates to the kitchen, wrapped foil around mine, and put it in the refrigerator for later. Ty'ree had pretty much finished his.

I sat on the couch and tried not to think of anything while Ty'ree got dressed. The rain was tapping hard against the window. Like somebody trying to get my attention. Like somebody trying to get inside.

EIGHT

ME AND TY'REE WALKED THE FOUR BLOCKS TO the train station without saying anything. He bought me two tokens using a bunch of change in his pocket. He had a MetroCard for himself since he went to work every day. The MetroCard let him ride the train as much as he liked for just a one-time charge. As he stood there counting out the change, I remembered him and Mama at the dining-room table adding and re-adding and trying to make the money go further than it was likely to go. I stood at the token booth with my hands in my pockets trying not to notice the people standing in line behind Ty'ree getting impatient.

When the train finally came, I took a seat by the window and stared out at the rainy darkness until the train went back into the tunnel and took us downtown.

I tried not to think about how poor we were, but when we got off at Fourteenth Street and walked up the stairs, all the lights from the stores hit me. There were toys and clothes in the windows and people dressed in nice warm coats and hats or getting out of fancy cars. As we walked along Fourteenth Street, I remembered the first time I realized we were poor. I was in third grade and my teacher gave everybody in the class a letter to take home. When Mama got home from work that night, I gave her the letter and sat beside her on the couch while she read it. I tried to read over her shoulder, but there were a lot of words typed real small. After Mama finished reading the letter, she folded it up—again and again until it was real tiny.

"If your teacher asks about it," she said, taking the letter to the kitchen and putting it in the trash, "you tell her we don't need anybody's Fresh Air Fund. You tell her we appreciate her thoughts though. You hear me, Lafayette?"

I had followed her as far as the kitchen doorway and stood there leaning against it nodding, not sure what she was talking about.

"What's Fresh Air Fund?" I asked.

Mama sighed and started washing the dishes left over from breakfast. She ran some hot water over them then rubbed Ivory soap on a washcloth before answering.

"It's a camp," she said.

"I *want* to go to camp."

"It's a camp for kids whose parents can't afford to send them somewhere else. For poor kids."

I watched Mama wash dishes and let the words sink in.

"Are we *poor*?" I asked.

"Poor enough," Mama said. She scratched her forehead with her soapy hand, then wiped the soap away with her arm. "But not that poor. And we won't always be this way, either."

When I was a baby, we all went to Bayamón, Puerto Rico, for my grandmother's funeral. Ty'ree said Puerto Rico was like what pictures of Paradise look like—all green and warm and pure. Mama always promised we'd go back again one summer when we had enough money.

"We ain't ever gonna have enough money," Charlie had said.

"Yes we will, Charlie," Mama told him. She pressed her hand against his cheek.

"When?" I asked, wanting to feel her hand on *my* cheek. Wanting her to look in *my* eyes and promise we'd have enough money.

"Soon," Mama said, still keeping her hand on Charlie's cheek. "Soon."

But it seemed most days we barely had enough money to pay the rent, let alone fly to Paradise.

"Soon ain't coming soon enough," Charlie said.

We were poorer now. Sometimes if Ty'ree didn't figure money out right or if something came up—like the time I lost three textbooks and had to pay for them before I could get new ones—we'd end up having stuff I didn't much care to eat, like cornbread that Ty'ree stretched with flour, and powdered vegetable soup with pieces of hot dogs in it. Or sometimes Ty'ree would send me to the store around the corner for seventy-five cents' worth of spiced ham and fifty cents' worth of cheese—enough for two sandwiches, three if you cut the meat in half and used a lot of mayonnaise. We got food stamps from the city and a little bit of money once a month, but there was always something one of us needed that seemed to cost just a little bit more than we had.

"You wish we were rich, T?"

Ty'ree nodded. "Every day. Maybe not *every* day, but most days."

"How come?"

"Life would just be easier. I could go to school."

Me and Ty'ree walked by a group of boys passing a bottle around on the corner of Fourteenth Street and Sixth Avenue. I eyed them, and one of them eyed me back, then said, "W's up." Me and Ty'ree said what's up back. They reminded me of Newcharlie and his friends hanging out on the corner of my block. I'd seen them in the same position—huddled in a circle passing a bottle of beer around. I wondered if that's what New-charlie was doing right now. I missed him suddenly. He'd never come with us to see an art flick, though. He said they bored the living mess out of him.

"It ain't *my* fault you're not in college, you know."

"Nobody's blaming anybody, Laf," Ty'ree said, sounding tired and old. "You just asked a question and I answered it. That's all."

It had stopped raining and gotten a little bit colder out now. I pulled my coat sleeves down over my hands. A limousine drove past us slowly, and I wondered if there was a famous rapper inside. Rappers and basket-ball players were always talking about buying their mamas houses and cars. If Newcharlie became a rap-per, I wondered what he'd buy us. I looked down at my boots. They were black and scuffed. Ty'ree had promised he'd have some money to get me another pair in two weeks. The boots felt kind of tight too. They made me remember that guy David and the shoehorn.

After Mama died, we started getting some money from the state. I think we got some when Daddy died too, but I'm not sure. When the checks came, Ty'ree usually used them to pay rent and buy food. He used the money he made at work to buy us clothes and school supplies. After the textbook thing he started trying to put a little in the bank for hard times. Some-times I sat at the dining-room table with him and helped him figure stuff out. By the time we got through figuring, there wasn't much left over. On pay-days, if the rent wasn't due, Ty'ree always made sure there was some left to see a movie or rent a video. And sometimes we'd stop at McDonald's or get a slice of pizza. I looked at Ty'ree. He was walking with his head down and frowning, like he was thinking serious about things. He needed a haircut, so his hair kind of fell toward his forehead a little. I looked down at his sneakers. They were old and dirty-looking. He'd bought them before Mama died. They were Adidas but the kind nobody wore anymore. I moved a little bit closer to him, wondering if people could tell we were poor. He *couldn't* go back to school. Not right now anyway. Because of me. Because of Newcharlie. He couldn't quit his job, and he couldn't go at night 'cause the caseworker would be on us talking about how me and Newcharlie were home alone too much. The only way he'd be able to go to college was if me and Newcharlie went to live down south.

"I don't like being poor, T."

Ty'ree looked at me. "We won't always be this way. You know that. It's just a temp thing."

He put his arm around my shoulder and I nodded. But I didn't see a way out. Just years and years of us this way. Us moving in a circle. A circle called Time.

"Ty'ree," I said. "That guy David from Rahway? He ever killed anybody with that shoehorn?" I wanted to change the subject, to stop thinking about being poor.

Ty'ree thought for a moment. "That's the story Charlie tells about the guy making a knife out of it?"

I nodded.

"Correction officer found it under his bed. That kid's probably still doing time."

"Newchar—I mean *Charlie* tries to make it seem like he killed someone."

"You ever try to just talk to Charlie?" Ty'ree asked. We turned onto Thirteenth Street.

I shrugged. "And say *what*?"

"You know, just talk. Say w's up. Ask him how his life is going. What kind of things he likes to do. Stuff like that."

"I know where his life is going—down the toilet."

Ty'ree eyed me. "Maybe he knows you think that and that's why he acts the way he does."

I felt myself starting to shake. I *hated* when Ty'ree did this. "It's not *my* fault!" I said. "Everything ain't my fault, all right?"

Some people turned to look at me, but I didn't care. I started walking fast down Thirteenth Street, past the Quad. Ty'ree was somewhere behind me. I didn't care. I hoped he would turn into dust. Hoped he would disappear. Forever and ever amen. I sniffed. I could feel tears running down my nose.

"Lafayette!" Ty'ree's hand was on my shoulder, yanking me around.

"It ain't my fault," I said, my voice choking up in the back of my throat. "He burned all of Mama's pictures!" I felt cold suddenly, cold and sweaty at the same time. I hated Newcharlie and I hated Ty'ree. I wanted to be dead. Dead like Mama. Maybe I'd die of hypothermia. Then it'd just be the two of them in that house, every day thinking about what they could have done to keep *me* alive.

"Just sat in the window and lit a match to them and let the little—" I gulped. I couldn't catch my breath. "He . . . he let the little fires float down."

A man with a little girl looked at us, then grabbed the little girl's hand and crossed the street.

"He didn't mean it, Lafayette." Ty'ree kept his hand on my shoulder. When I tried to jerk away, he held tighter. "It was just his way—"

"Those two pictures I got are the only ones left." I hated Newcharlie. *Hated* him. "Wish he'd never come home. Least then we'd have some other pictures."

"I know," he said. "I know."

I felt myself sagging into Ty'ree like he was a wall, felt him put his arms around me. "Then he got the nerve to put plants in all the windows, Ty'ree. Like plants was gonna change something."

"I know, Laf," Ty'ree kept saying. "I know."

"He's all bad, T," I cried. "And you're all good and I ain't nothing."

Ty'ree let out a little laugh. "Nah, Lafayette. Charlie ain't all bad. And you know you got it going on." He was quiet for a moment. "And I . . . I *definitely* am not all good."

I was getting colder and colder. Ty'ree kept his arms around me to keep me from shivering.

"Brother to brother, Lafayette?"

I nodded. "B to B," I whispered. It was something Ty'ree had started saying right after Mama died. It meant I love you, but we'd never really said that to each other. He'd said brother to brother meant that and then some. It meant we'd be there for each other, no matter what.

"Hey, let's bag the movie and go get something hot to drink, okay?" Ty'ree said.

"Yeah. Let's." Ty'ree kept his arm around my shoulder as we walked back toward Sixth Avenue. We went into a coffee shop on the corner of Sixth and Tenth. There weren't that many people in it, and me and Ty'ree took seats in the back. There was soft music playing and a couple of people sitting at tables writing in notebooks and on laptop computers. I ordered a hot chocolate and an apple Danish, and Ty'ree ordered coffee. He handed me his napkin, and I wiped my eyes and blew my nose. I felt tired. Tired and empty, and even with Ty'ree right across the table from me, I felt a little bit alone.

Our stuff came and Ty'ree started talking. I picked at my Danish, hoping he'd tell me about Mama, about the day she died. I hoped he'd change the story around and make me the hero, the one who saved her. But he didn't. He started talking about our daddy. And when he started talking, we weren't in that coffee shop anymore. We were in Central Park. I stopped picking at my Danish and leaned in close. Not wanting to miss any of it.

NINE

"LOOK HERE, TY'REE," DADDY SAID. HE HELD the newspaper out so Ty'ree could get a look at the words there. "Says maybe the Knicks are gonna win this year. That'll be something new, huh?"

Ty'ree climbed over the park bench, then climbed back to the side Daddy was on. He was ten, in fourth grade, and probably the best climber in the whole school. He wanted Daddy to see him, to watch him hang off the side of the bench like a monkey. He climbed up to the back and walked along the edge of it like it was a high wire. When he stepped over

Daddy's head, Daddy glanced up and smiled. It was Sunday, cold enough to see your breath. They always came to Central Park on Sundays. Mama was at home taking care of Charlie and getting ready for the new baby that was coming. Ty'ree wanted a sister, 'cause he'd already gotten a brother and that wasn't all it was cracked up to be. Daddy'd said he wanted another boy 'cause you couldn't have too many boys. When he said this, Mama laughed and swatted him with whatever was close by. Mama said she got down on her knees and prayed for a girl some nights 'cause she didn't know what she'd do if another little man showed up in her house. When they were laughing and teasing about the baby, Ty'ree didn't care if it ever came, just so long as his mama and daddy could keep on laughing and having a good time. He figured his mama was probably about the prettiest woman in Manhattan. People said he looked just like her but he didn't see himself as pretty. He hoped his new baby sister would be pretty like Mama.

"Look, Daddy," Ty'ree said. He was a few feet away from his father now, high up in a leafless oak tree. Seemed he could look out and see the whole park from where he sat. Maybe if he went up higher, he could see the whole world.

"You sure can climb," Daddy said, then went back to reading the paper.

It was cold out, and the air seemed to lift up under the heavy coat Ty'ree was wearing. He loved being cold. It made him feel electrified. He loved feeling electrified. He sat down on a branch and let his feet dangle over the edge. His sneakers were white and new, and he promised himself he'd never get them dirty.

There were only a few other people in the park. Way down, there was a man playing with two little kids, running in circles and making them chase him. The kids were squealing and grabbing at his coat. He kept dodging them. There was a woman in a pink running outfit jogging around the lake. She had a big dog with her, and the dog was running right beside her. Ty'ree wished he could get a dog. Maybe a mastiff. He'd seen one once. That was probably the biggest dog in the world. He'd even settle for a Doberman.

Ty'ree heard somebody screaming. When he looked out toward the frozen lake, he saw the dog that had been running with the woman skidding out on the lake. He held his breath. Even from where he sat, he could hear the deep crackle of the ice. "Daddy!" he screamed. The dog kicked out its front legs, then its back. Then it was sinking. "Daddy!" Ty'ree called

again. The dog gave a yelp and disappeared under-
neath the water for a moment. Then the woman was
running out onto the ice, screaming. Then she too was
disappearing and reappearing, disappearing and reap-
pearing.

Ty'ree jumped down from the tree and ran over to
his father, who was standing now and staring out at
the water.

"You gotta help them, Daddy," Ty'ree said, out of
breath. "Daddy, that dog . . . that dog and lady . . ."

But his daddy was already running toward the
water. Ty'ree watched his father break a branch off a
tree and hold it out to the woman. But the branch
snapped when the woman reached for it. Then his fa-
ther was running along the icy bank and slipping
slowly into the water. Ty'ree screamed. The man who
had been playing with the two kids was standing a
bit away from him, holding a kid in each arm and
shouting something.

"Then Daddy was pulling the woman and the dog
out of the water," Ty'ree said. "And far away I could
hear sirens." He looked down at his hands. "Sirens and
my own self screaming."

TEN

I STARED AT THE BOTTOM OF MY EMPTY CUP.
Ty'ree had stopped talking, but I couldn't look at him.
Not right away. Nobody had ever told me that he was
right there watching our daddy slip into that frozen
pond. Everybody had known it, but nobody had told
me. It was like a secret—a lie that had been in my life
since before I was born.

I could hear people talking all around us. Talking
and laughing. I tried to imagine my daddy running
out into that pond, but I couldn't. I could only see
Ty'ree there, screaming from under that tree.

"How come y'all never told me?" I whispered. I wanted to scream it, but I didn't know what the words would do. Maybe they'd just sink into the walls and disappear. Maybe they'd reappear years and years later—in front of some boy who had spent his whole life thinking otherwise.

"Why?" Ty'ree asked.

I looked up at him to see if he was serious. What'd he mean, *why*? 'Cause I was his brother. 'Cause it was my daddy. 'Cause it mattered.

" 'Cause," I said. "Just 'cause."

"You think it would have made a difference if you had grown up knowing that I was there?"

I nodded.

"Why?"

"How come you asking why, Ty'ree? You must've known it would've made some difference, 'cause y'all decided not to tell me. I'm not *stupid*."

"You know how you always want to know what were the last words I said to Mama?" Ty'ree asked.

I nodded.

"Well, it always makes me think of the last words I said to Daddy."

"You know what they were?"

"Yeah. The lady was in shock when the ambulance

77

got there. But Daddy was okay, so they let him and me go home."

Ty'ree swallowed and looked away from me. He stared around the restaurant a minute before going on. "They gave him this blanket to wear even though he kept insisting he was fine in all those wet clothes. But he put the blanket on anyway and the cops drove us home. Mama nearly went crazy when she saw him. She was scared something had happened to me."

"Where was Charlie?"

"By the time we got home, Mama'd put him down for a nap."

He got quiet again. I waited, and when he started talking, his voice was real low.

"After Daddy got out of those wet clothes and climbed into bed, I came into the room. I asked him if he thought the dog was going to be okay." Ty'ree smiled. It was the saddest smile I'd ever seen in my life.

"Then what happened?"

"Daddy said, 'It's all right, T. I'm warm now. I'm warm now.' "

Ty'ree shook his head.

"I wouldn't talk about it for a long time. Charlie used to always ask me about what happened, but I wouldn't say. And I made Mama promise not to talk about it. I wanted to make believe I wasn't there. Figured if nobody talked about it, I wouldn't go around blaming myself 'cause I had told Daddy to help them. And you know why I told him to help them?"

I shook my head. Something was coming to me—slow and clear as pancake syrup. Charlie, I kept thinking. Charlie.

" 'Cause I wanted a stupid dog!" Ty'ree said. "I wanted a dog more than anything in the world, and because of it I lost my dad. You know what that does to you?"

"Yeah," I whispered. But Ty'ree didn't hear me. "He would've gone in there anyway," I said a little bit louder. "Right?"

Ty'ree shrugged and kept looking around the restaurant. He was sort of bobbing his head, like he was hearing music inside it. The waitress came over and asked us if we wanted anything else. When Ty'ree didn't say anything, I ordered two refills.

Sometimes I stared in the mirror and was surprised to see how little and lost I looked. That was how Ty'ree looked now—like he was waiting for somebody to come and take his hand and show him the way home.

"How come Charlie didn't go to the park with you?"

Ty'ree kept bobbing his head. "Too small," he said, still looking out at the restaurant. "Daddy wanted to read his paper. Didn't want to have to keep an eye out for him. Sundays were me and Daddy's time.

"The thing is," Ty'ree said, "Charlie wasn't there for any of it—for Daddy, for Mama. And it's made him mad. Mad and helpless."

I shook my head again, trying to shake Charlie thoughts out of it, but I couldn't. All those years Charlie must have grown up watching Mama and Ty'ree at the table trying to figure out how to keep us eating and wearing clothes, and him not being able to help. All those years of him being too small or too much trouble. Him not being the one Daddy wanted to take to the park.

I looked around the coffee shop. There were a lot of people in it now. A woman was sitting in one corner by herself reading a magazine. I wondered if she'd ever been jogging in Central Park. Wondered if she'd ever had or wanted a dog or had a brother who was mad all the way down to his bones.

"We got all this stuff to carry around with us,"

Ty'ree said "You know how they say drug addicts got a monkey on their back?"

"Nah."

"Well, that's what people say. And it's like we got monkeys on our backs, except it ain't drugs."

"You wanted that dog," I said. "And I wanted some breakfast. Just regular stuff people want. We didn't know what was gonna happen or anything. Charlie didn't want anything from them . . . I don't think. I mean, maybe he just wanted them—maybe he wanted Daddy to take him to the park and you and Mama to let him help with stuff. But that ain't no monkey."

The waitress brought us refills, and Ty'ree waited till she left again before he started talking.

"Yeah, it is," he said. "Charlie got the biggest monkey on his back. I can remember the last thing I said to Daddy and you can remember the last thing you said to Mama. Least we got to be there. But not Charlie. And I think he carries that around. It's more like a gorilla on his back than a monkey."

"Nobody told him to go hold up that store," I said.

"But he did," Ty'ree said. "And while he was gone, me and you had each other after Mama died. And he just had Rahway, you know."

"It turned him mad," I said.

Ty'ree nodded. "And I don't know where he's gonna take that mad," he said. "I really don't."

"Should send him to Dr. Vernon," I said. "That shrink y'all sent me to."

Ty'ree shook his head. "We don't have Dr. Vernon money anymore. And Charlie said he didn't want to go to a psychologist—said he had to see one when he was in Rahway. And since he hasn't really gotten into trouble again, I can't make him."

"But he's evil incarnate," I said. I kept thinking about the way Newcharlie's face twisted up every time he called me Milagros killer. It reminded me of somebody possessed.

"*Evil incarnate?*" Ty'ree smiled and shook his head. "You'll probably grow up to write those thriller movies where everyone's always screaming."

"If I have to keep living with Newcharlie, I will. I'll have firsthand experience."

ELEVEN

TY'REE WAS ALL RIGHT AFTER MAMA DIED. BUT I was all wrong. The year before, I'd seen this show about snakes. They showed this one snake slipping out of its old skin and then leaving that old skin on the ground behind him. That's how I felt—like Mama'd been my skin. But I hadn't grown a new skin underneath, like that snake had. I was just blood and bones spreading all over the place. Every night Ty'ree stayed with me in my room till I cried myself to sleep. And the next morning he'd find me sleeping curled up on the floor beside his bed.

After a few weeks of me ending up on the floor, he called Aunt Cecile, and she came back to New York and asked around trying to find a doctor I could go to—a psychologist. Some afternoons I'd come home from school to find Aunt Cecile sitting at the dining-room table writing down and crossing out numbers as she talked on the phone. And some evenings I'd catch her and Ty'ree whispering about different doctors, their fees, and social service benefits.

Then one afternoon Aunt Cecile announced that she'd found a person I could talk to named Dr. Vernon. That Wednesday and for a whole lot of Wednesdays after that, Aunt Cecile would take me to Dr. Vernon— an old man with a nice office in Harlem. His office was all wood and windows and smelled like heat and dust and warm blankets. Smells I'd always liked. So while Aunt Cecile sat in the waiting room, I went into Dr. Vernon's office. I wasn't afraid, 'cause the warm-blanket smell felt like it was covering me up, protecting me.

The first time I went to Dr. Vernon, he put some paper and some markers on his desk and asked me to draw a picture for him. There was a little table in the corner, and he told me I could sit there and draw for as long as I liked. But I didn't want to draw. I sat at that table for a long time just feeling the warm blanket around me and staring at that blank white paper and those markers until Dr. Vernon told me it was okay to go.

The second time I went, Dr. Vernon gave me the paper and the markers again. I wrote my name in blue. *Lafayette Miguel Bailey.* Then I wrote Ty'ree's whole name, which is Ty'ree Alfonso Bailey. And Charlie's name, Charles Javier Bailey. I stared at the paper until Dr. Vernon came over to see. He was tall and thin the way Ty'ree said my daddy had been. But Dr. Vernon's hair was white like Aunt Cecile's. And he had a white beard—a skinny black Santa Claus. I stared at the paper, and I could feel him standing above me staring down at it, too.

"That's your family," he said.

I shrugged.

"Any other members?"

I shook my head.

"How does that make you feel?" Dr. Vernon asked.

I shrugged again. "Like nothing."

"You feel like you're nothing, Lafayette?"

"No. I know I'm something. I'm just saying that not having a mama and a daddy don't feel like nothing. It's just the way things are."

"And how does that make you feel?" he asked again.

I stared down at the paper, at me and my brothers' names. It was a lot of white space where there wasn't any writing. I had tried to write our names real big, but they still looked small, almost like nothing against all that white.

"I want my mama back," I whispered.

Dr. Vernon patted me on the shoulder and said, "I know you do, Lafayette."

We stayed like that a long time—me staring down at the paper, Dr. Vernon softly patting my shoulder. We didn't say anything. There wasn't anything to say. After a long while had passed, Dr. Vernon said, "You can go now, Lafayette."

But I didn't want to go. I liked the way it felt to have Dr. Vernon patting my shoulder. I liked how deep and soft his voice was. So I came back. Every Wednesday for a whole year. And while Dr. Vernon stood above me or sat beside me, I drew pictures and told him what I remembered and what I wished for. I told him about the hairy hands that came at my throat in the middle of the night, the hands that wanted to choke me for not saving Mama. And how the only way I could keep them away from me was to go into

Mama's room, where she was waiting for me, where she told me to lie down and go to sleep, that everything would be all right soon.

"What does 'all right' mean, Lafayette?" Dr. Vernon asked me one Wednesday. By then Aunt Cecile had long gone back down south, and I took the train by myself. I'd gotten used to the train ride, to Dr. Vernon's wood-and-window office, to his soft voice telling me all the things I'd done right in my life and how it wasn't my fault Mama had died.

I looked down at the picture I'd been drawing. It was a picture of me and Ty'ree walking together down our block. Ty'ree had his hand around my shoulder and was smiling. I had my hands in my pockets and was looking up at him.

I held the picture up so Dr. Vernon could get a closer look at it. "This," I said, feeling a smile coming on.

"If you're scared at night—" Dr. Vernon began, but I didn't let him finish.

"Then Ty'ree's there for me. Ty'ree and Mama."

"Where's your mama, Lafayette?" Dr. Vernon asked softly. His white eyebrows crinkled, and he looked at me like he was searching my face for something.

"She died," I whispered. "I know that. But I still feel her."

"Where?"

"Everywhere."

I looked at Dr. Vernon. It was almost time to go. He'd told me a while back that this would be my last visit with him, that I'd done all the work I needed to do here. He said I was gonna be okay.

Dr. Vernon smiled and patted my shoulder. "You can go now, Lafayette. Maybe I'll see you around sometime."

"Yeah," I said. When I got to the door, I turned to him and waved good-bye, then ran back over and hugged him hard. "Maybe," I said.

TWELVE

IT WAS ONLY A LITTLE BIT AFTER TEN WHEN ME
and Ty'ree got back Friday night. The apartment was
dark, which meant Newcharlie hadn't come home. He
didn't have to be home until eleven thirty on Friday
and Saturday, and most times he squeezed in right as
the second hand was moving toward eleven forty-five.
Ty'ree didn't fuss with him about that. A long time
ago Ty'ree had said he was going to choose his argu-
ments with Newcharlie or else they'd be fighting
every minute of the day. Even though people call him
St. Ty'ree, he's not really. He's flesh and blood and

makes mistakes just like other people. Once I saw him push this man out of his way when he was running for the train. It was like he didn't even see the man as a human being. And the year before, when his girlfriend dumped him, he was just pure evil to live with for a while. And not telling me till now that he'd been there when my daddy went in that lake. Nah, he wasn't *all* good.

We'd gotten a video, and I put it in the VCR and went to get the rest of my dinner from the refrigerator. Ty'ree checked the messages. There was one from a girl he kind of liked, so he went into his room and called her back. He dated girls off and on, and some of them were okay and some of them were dumb. I hadn't met this new one yet. It took Ty'ree a while before he brought a girl he was dating home. He was private that way. Mostly they went out to movies or met on his lunch break. Sometimes he went to their house. Girls acted like he was *God* or something when they learned he was raising me and Newcharlie. St. Ty'ree.

"Yo, T!" I yelled. "You gonna watch the movie?"

I heard Ty'ree telling the girl to hold on. "You go ahead," he called to me. I heard him close the door to his room.

I sat there wishing Smitty and PJ were around even if Smitty *was* nosy. I *hadn't* changed like Ty'ree said. I just didn't want to answer a whole lot of questions. "Mama," I whispered, "I'm still me. I'm still Lafayette."

Me and Mama used to sit watching movies till late. We'd usually get funny ones and sit there cracking up over the stupidest thing. I rubbed my hand over the couch cushion. Mama'd sit right there. And she'd laugh and laugh.

This movie was about a guy who wakes up one morning and can't tell any lies. He'd been lying to everyone, including his little son, for a long time. But this one day, every time he opened his mouth, the truth came out and he found himself saying stuff he hadn't meant to say. It was supposed to be a comedy, but it wasn't that funny. I ate my chicken and watched the movie, wondering what it would mean if the whole world woke up having to tell the truth. Maybe then I would have known a long time ago about Ty'ree being at that lake with my daddy.

It was one of those movies you can figure out the end of by the time you get to the middle. I watched it a little more than halfway through, then washed my plate, changed into a T-shirt and shorts, brushed my teeth, and went to bed. Ty'ree was still on the phone. It was a little bit after eleven thirty. I fell asleep listening for Newcharlie's footsteps on the stairs.

IT WAS THE STUPID DOG THAT KEPT WAKING ME up. First the barking that wasn't really there. Three times I heard it. And each time I sat straight up in bed. Then nothing. Not even a whimper. But each time I turned over and started falling asleep again, the barking started up. Then, when I was almost asleep, I heard a car screech and slam into something. Something soft and solid.

"No!" I sat straight up again and blinked. The room was dark. "Uh-uh," I whispered. It had been a reddish dog, with long hair and dark, sad eyes. It kept trying to bark, but no sound came out. I swallowed. The dog had its head on Newcharlie's—no, on *Charlie's* lap.

I pulled the covers up over me and lay down again. My eyes felt heavy and dry. But when I closed them, it wasn't sleep that came to me but Charlie. Charlie with his face raised up toward the sky howling, screaming to nobody, *Please, God, don't let it die.*

THIRTEEN

"LAFAYETTE."

The dog was gone and Charlie was gone and I was at that stream near Aunt Cecile's house again. It was pretty out, the sun cutting its way around the leaves and dancing up off the water. I had a big trout on the end of my line, and it was fighting hard. Every time it came up, I saw the colors dancing off its scales. It had an angry mouth and devil eyes. But that whole head would be gone soon, and I'd be picking my teeth with its bones.

"Lafayette, wake up."

Then the trout was talking, calling my name and shaking me. Then it was disappearing downstream. Then the stream was gone. But the fish was still calling my name.

"Lafayette."

I opened my eyes to see Ty'ree standing above me. The room was almost dark. There was just the tiniest bit of light in it, like maybe it was five in the morning or earlier. I rubbed my eyes and tried to turn away from Ty'ree, but he shook me again.

"They got Charlie," he whispered.

"The dog got him?"

"Lafayette," Ty'ree said, his voice just a little bit louder than before. "C'mon and wake up. The police got him. We have to go down to the station."

"You go."

Ty'ree switched on the light and I jumped up. My head felt like it was gonna fly off from all the brightness.

"Nah, man," Ty'ree said. "Brother to brother."

I wanted to say, *Brother to brother my butt*, but I was too tired. Ty'ree handed me my pants and shirt at the same time. He was still wearing the clothes he'd had on the night before.

"Police got him for what?" I asked, pulling the pants on over my shorts. "The dog?" Things in my head were all fuzzy. Charlie was holding a dog. I was fishing. Had he stolen the dog? Is that why the police had him?

"What dog?"

I shook my head. "Nothing," I said, remembering. "It was a dream, I think. What'd they get him for?"

"I don't know. He just called, said I need to go down there." Ty'ree cursed and went back into his bedroom. I could hear him opening and closing drawers. The hallway light was on, and I saw him walk back past my room on his way to the living room.

"Hurry up, Laf," he said.

When I came into the living room, Ty'ree was pulling his keys off the nail by the door and pulling on his raincoat at the same time. I hadn't noticed before, but now I saw that the rain was coming down hard and steady. I went back to my room and got my rain slicker. The sleeves were too short, but otherwise it was fine.

We walked out into the early-morning darkness without saying anything. I wanted to tell Ty'ree that Newcharlie always found a way to mess up, but he had his head down and his hands in his pockets. His face was all bunched up like he was thinking the exact same thing, so I walked beside him and kept my mouth shut.

FOURTEEN

I'D NEVER BEEN INSIDE A POLICE STATION BE-
fore, and when we got there, I felt like I was gonna be
sick. There were fluorescent lights everywhere, but
the place still seemed dark, like the inside of a cave. I
tried to breathe through my mouth—there was a
smell to the place, like something or someone had died
inside its walls. Everywhere I looked, there were desks
that were so huge and dark, you could barely see the
people sitting behind them, and people moving in and
out of offices—mostly cops. It felt like a place where it

was always gray and rainy. Like it was always Judgment Day.

A skinny man sitting high up like a judge looked down at me and Ty'ree and asked if he could help us. Ty'ree told him why we were there, and the man pointed us down a hall.

Ty'ree reached to take my hand and I snatched it back. He blinked, like he was realizing I was twelve, not six, and walked ahead of me. Phones were ringing and people were calling out information to each other. A woman at the end of the hall said Newcharlie's name. Me and Ty'ree walked faster.

Once I saw a woman faint on the subway, and when I saw Newcharlie, that's just what I felt like doing. I felt my head get light and my arms go numb. Ty'ree saw him at the same time and broke into a run down the hall. Newcharlie was sitting on a bench curled up into the corner like he wanted to disappear. His lip was busted and one of his eyes was swollen completely shut. His hands were trembling like he was cold. The right one was cut and swollen big as a bear paw.

That's my brother, I wanted to shout. *What'd y'all do to my brother?*

Instead, I bit my bottom lip and stood back while

Ty'ree went to him. When Ty'ree sat down on the bench next to him, Newcharlie tried to move away, but there wasn't anyplace to go.

"Yo," Ty'ree whispered.

I heard something jangle and looked at Newcharlie's hands again. He was wearing handcuffs.

He looked at me out of his one good eye. I looked at him back, and for a long time every sound in the world disappeared. *Don't die on us, Charlie,* I wanted to say. I wanted to run to him and throw my arms around his shoulders. But I just stood there, biting my lip and looking into his one good eye. *When someone hurts you,* Charlie said to me once, *you just hold on. Hold on until the pain goes away.* We were little then, and a kid from school had punched me in the eye for accidentally stepping on his toe. I hadn't learned how to fight and didn't want to anyway, so I waited in the school yard until Charlie came out. He'd been playing basketball with some other guys in the gym, so when he finally came out of the school building, the school yard was empty and my eye had swollen shut. *The pain always goes away, Laf. You just hold on, you hear me?* He put his arm around me and we walked on home. And slowly the pain went away.

Ty'ree touched the swollen eye and Newcharlie

jerked back and frowned. Then Ty'ree touched his lip, real gentle, and Newcharlie let him.

"It's okay," Ty'ree whispered.

You just hold on, Charlie. The pain always goes away.

Ty'ree kept telling Newcharlie it was gonna be okay. It felt like the moment had frozen, like we were all stuck that way—me standing a little bit away from them, Ty'ree looking like he wanted to hug Newcharlie but was scared to and Newcharlie doing everything he could not to cry.

"I ain't do nothing, T," Newcharlie whispered, his words coming out slow and muffled because of his lip. "I swear I didn't. I didn't know nothing about it. I swear I didn't steal that car."

"What car?" Ty'ree asked. "What happened, Charlie?"

I took a step closer to hear him better, and just as I did, a policeman came over to us.

"He yours?" he asked Ty'ree. He was a tall black guy with glasses. The pin above his badge said "Joseph." I looked from his pin to his face.

"My brother," Ty'ree said, standing up. "I'm the legal guardian. Ty'ree Bailey." He took some papers from his pocket and handed them to the cop. The papers were from the state, saying that Ty'ree had custody of me and Newcharlie. I'd seen them a couple of times before.

The cop read them slowly, nodding as he did. "He was in a stolen car," he said, not looking up from the papers. "Him and another guy. Mr. Bailey here wasn't driving." He looked at Ty'ree and frowned. "They got the guy who was driving in a holding pen back there. Broke his parole. So did your brother."

I swallowed and looked down at my sneakers, trying not to think about Newcharlie going to jail and me going to Aunt Cecile's.

"He said he ain't know about the car," I whispered.

Ty'ree and Officer Joseph looked at me.

"My brother say he ain't—he *didn't* steal the car," I said.

"No, he didn't." Officer Joseph handed the papers back to Ty'ree. "He got banged up pretty bad though. I'll let him tell you about that."

Newcharlie was crying softly in the corner.

"Is that what happened to his face?" Ty'ree asked. The muscles in his jaw were moving back and forth the way they did when he was trying to hold his temper.

Officer Joseph sighed and shook his head. He took

a key ring from his pocket and walked over to New-charlie, undid the handcuffs, and clipped them to his holster.

"He'll tell you what happened," he said, looking at Newcharlie. "Mr. Bailey knows the rules. He knows he breaks his parole, he goes to jail. He knows you go to an initiation, you're going to have to fight." He shook his head and turned back to Ty'ree. "Last thing I want to do is send another young brother to jail. I'm going to let you take him home this time, but I don't want to see him in my precinct again. Not unless he's working here."

Ty'ree nodded. "Thank you, sir."

"Thank you, sir," I whispered.

Newcharlie put his head down and walked out the door without saying anything.

"WHAT THE HELL HAPPENED?" TY'REE ASKED when we were a block from the precinct, his questions coming fast. "What's that officer talking about? Why you gotta mess up, Charlie?" He pushed Charlie. "You always the one gotta mess up. Me and Lafayette—"

"Stop it, Ty'ree," I said. "Stop it!"

Ty'ree clenched his hands.

"I'm always the one," Newcharlie said. "The bad one. The loser. That's me. The one who always messes up. Ain't it always been that way?"

"Yes," Ty'ree said. The muscles in his jaw were working fast. "It's always been that way."

"I ain't never gonna be anything," Newcharlie said. "So why even try?"

I swallowed, and Ty'ree looked down at his hands. We walked a long way in silence, Newcharlie walking a little bit ahead of us with his head still down.

"You don't always mess up, Cha," I said.

"Yes I do. And you're the angel. The innocent one. The one everybody gotta look out for. I ain't nothing. Nobody."

It was daylight out now. The sky was pretty—gray blue from the rain. Newcharlie wasn't wearing a raincoat. Ty'ree had tried to give him his, but Newcharlie wouldn't take it. His clothes were dripping wet. Maybe he wanted to die of hypothermia.

"Why you have to do this, huh, Charlie?" Ty'ree said. "Why you gotta do this to us?"

"I ain't do anything, T."

Ty'ree's jaw was working fast. He clenched and unclenched his fists. *Don't hit him*, I kept thinking. *Don't.*

I'd seen Ty'ree lose it and hit Newcharlie once. That night the cops came to our place. Just as they were taking Charlie away, Ty'ree jumped off the couch and punched him in the back. Then both of them started bawling.

"I ain't steal that car, Ty'ree," Newcharlie said.

Maybe Ty'ree couldn't see it but I could. There was something real sad about Newcharlie right then. It was that same look he'd had that day the vet told him that dog had died. The same look he had the day we buried Mama. He looked . . . broken.

"You ain't a nobody, Cha," I said, but I don't think either of them heard me.

Ty'ree cursed again. He was madder than I'd seen him in a long time. "What the hell were you doing in it? And what were you doing fighting in the street?" He took a quick step and grabbed Newcharlie by the shoulder and swung him around. Newcharlie tried to frown, but his lips were trembling. "You don't give a damn about anybody but yourself, do you? You mess up, Lafayette goes to Cecile and you go to jail. Is that what you want, man?"

Newcharlie shook his head. He was crying full out now. "I didn't know anything. Aaron and me—we went to this party. Only it wasn't a party, it was—it was an initiation."

Ty'ree pushed him, hard. "What are—"

"Stop, T." I tried to shout, but my voice was soft and high, like a scared little kid's. I looked around, nervous. But there was nobody else on the street.

Ty'ree stopped pushing him and glared at me.

"What're you talking about, Charlie? You better talk to me, 'cause I don't have a lot of patience for your junk tonight. I'm about ready to send both of you packing."

"For the Fordhams," Newcharlie said.

"The what?"

"It's a gang, T," I said.

Ty'ree looked like he didn't know if he wanted to smack me or Newcharlie first.

"What—?"

"I just thought it was a party," Newcharlie said. "I didn't know Aaron was in no gang. I thought he was lying. Then he showed me his colors. You had to fight somebody. I didn't want to do it, but—" He started choking. After a long time he had enough breath to talk again. "It makes you *somebody*. Aaron got all these other homeboys around him now. He don't really need me—" Newcharlie started gulping again. He put his head in both his hands like he was trying to hide inside them. "It makes you somebody. It gives you people."

"How'd you get in the car?" Ty'ree asked.

"I—I was—scared, T. This guy, this older guy, said he'd take me home. Aaron got in this other car, and he said I'd be all right. I thought it was cool. I just—I just wanted to go home. . . . Aaron said they'd just drive around a little bit. Said I didn't have to fight. But the guy—the guy in the car, he said I needed a couple of punches, toughen me up." Charlie swallowed, and opened and closed his mouth a couple of times like he was trying to drink the air. "I just wanted to go home," he whispered.

Ty'ree shook his head and looked off down the block. "Damn," he whispered.

"You in a gang now, Newcharlie?"

Ty'ree glared at me but I didn't care. If Newcharlie was in a gang now, he'd be the next one in our family to die. Gang members were always dying. I felt my bottom lip starting to tremble. I didn't know what I'd do if I lost somebody else.

But Newcharlie shook his head. "I ain't never going back."

"What happened to Aaron?" I asked.

Newcharlie shook his head again. "I don't know. I thought the cops got him, too, but they didn't." He pressed the cut on his swollen hand against his mouth and sucked it hard. There was a tiny cut on his cheek that I hadn't noticed before. I wondered what other bruises he had.

"I don't want to see Aaron nowhere near our place," Ty'ree said. "You hear me?"

Newcharlie nodded and wiped rain off of his face. "I didn't want to fight nobody," he kept whispering.

Ty'ree put his arm around Newcharlie's shoulder. His other hand was still clenching in and out of a fist. "C'mon," he said. "Let's get on out of this rain."

FIFTEEN

MAMA READ ALL THE TIME. WHEN SHE WASN'T reading to me, she was reading to herself. She'd always have one or two books in her bag 'cause she liked to read on the train going to work. We used to play a game where every day I'd ask her to name a book and then tell me the name of the person who wrote it. If it was one she'd said already, she'd have to give me a dollar. I earned one dollar in all of me and Mama's years of playing that game.

She liked to read this writer named Toni Morrison. Once she read me something Toni Morrison had written.

Listen to this, Lafayette, Mama said.

I was sitting across from her at the dining-room table, flipping through the pages of a comic book. I was probably eight or nine, and it was dark outside. Too dark for me to be out but not for Ty'ree and Charlie. So I was sitting there being a little bit mad, sitting right near her but not really caring about what she had to say.

"The function of freedom," Mama read, "is to free someone else."

I shrugged and went back to my comic book.

You ever thought about that, Laf? Mama asked me. *That being free means you help somebody else get free?*

I shook my head.

She put her book down.

Why not?

'Cause I ain't free.

Mama looked at me and frowned.

Well, I'm not, I said. *If I was free, then I'd be able to go outside like Ty'ree and Charlie.*

Then Mama laughed. But I didn't see what was so funny about the truth.

SIXTEEN

THE PHONE RANG IN THE LATE AFTERNOON. Ty'ree and Newcharlie were still asleep, but I'd been lying in bed talking to Mama, telling her about the precinct and how she didn't have to worry 'cause it was a place I never wanted to see the inside of again. She was sitting at the foot of my bed, rubbing my feet the way she would some nights when I couldn't fall asleep. *The way the lights were, Mama? It made you feel real sad inside. Like your life was over. Mama? Is Newcharlie's life over?*

"Somebody answer that!" Ty'ree yelled from his

room, his voice sounding sleepy and muffled like it was coming from underneath his pillow. Newcharlie groaned and turned over. His face was still swollen, even though Ty'ree had made him ice it when we got home.

Mama's hands faded from my feet; then her face was gone too. I stared at Newcharlie for a moment, my question hanging in the air over his bed. The phone rang two more times, and I got out of bed to get it.

"Yo, Lafayette? It's Smitty. What took you so long to answer, man?"

"Nothing. We still sleeping." I sat down at the dining-room table and squinted against the sun coming in through the windows. "What's up?"

"Why so late?"

"What's up?" I asked again, ignoring his question. I didn't want to give him anything to ask questions about.

"You feel like playing ball or something?" Smitty asked.

"I thought you was at your cousin's house for the weekend."

"Nah, man. My aunt said she was taking us all to church this afternoon, and me and PJ said we had to get home and catch up on schoolwork." Smitty laughed. "She's taking my cousin to church every weekend now, and he's like 'C'mon Smitty, it'll be fun.' I was out of there . . ."

I yawned and sat there in my underwear listening to Smitty go on for a while.

"You feel like going to the park?"

I pushed some leaves from one of Newcharlie's plants out of the way and looked out the window. "Yeah. I'll meet you downstairs in a few."

"Don't be taking a long time, Laf."

"I just gotta get dressed, man. Give me like twenty minutes."

"You said a few—"

"Okay, then forget about it—"

"Okay, okay. Twenty minutes. Jeez, man. Go back to bed and wake up on a better side."

He hung up, and I wrote a note for Ty'ree telling him where I was going, ate four pieces of bread with peanut butter, then went back into my room and pulled my pants on over my shorts. I sniffed under my arms, then thought better of it and went and took a quick shower. By the time I came back into the room, Newcharlie was sitting up in bed, touching his lip and frowning.

"Where you going?" he asked.

"Hang with Smitty and PJ—probably play ball."

"Yeah?"

"Yeah." I pulled my pants back on slowly, wishing I knew what to say. Wishing I knew how to free him.

Newcharlie looked at me for a moment like he was gonna say he was coming with us, but then he lay back down and turned toward the wall. I stood staring at his back, wishing he'd turn around and say he'd come.

He didn't, and I didn't know how to ask him.

SEVENTEEN

Smitty and PJ were sitting on my stoop rolling a basketball back and forth between them. PJ is two years younger than me and Smitty, small and quiet. Everyone called Smitty the pretty one on account of his dimples and straight teeth. Which I guess made PJ the ugly one, since he wore braces and didn't have dimples. I didn't think Smitty was all that easy to look at—not like the way grown people made a fuss over him.

Smitty stood up and brushed something off his overalls. They were new and stiff-looking. His aunt was rich and always buying them new stuff. PJ had on a new pair of sneakers. It wasn't that I was jealous that they had rich relatives, I just didn't think Smitty needed to be flashing his new stuff every minute. I was wearing a pair of pants that used to be New-charlie's and the green shirt Ty'ree had given me a long time ago.

"Yo," Smitty said. "I hear they got Charlie last night. He going back to Rahway?"

I took the ball from them and bounced it a couple of times, dribbling it back and forth between my legs.

"Might want to go on upstairs and ask him about that," I said, knowing full well that Smitty was scared of Newcharlie. Once Newcharlie'd caught him asking me questions about my daddy dying. He'd let Smitty know right off it wasn't any of his business. Not in a nice way, either.

Smitty glanced up at our window. "Nah," he said. "That's okay."

"Who'd you hear that from?" I tried to sound like I didn't care. I hated how fast news traveled around this neighborhood.

"Aaron told my cousin and my cousin told me. They really got Charlie?"

"Aaron should keep his mouth closed if he don't

know what he's talking about. Charlie ain't going back to Rahway. He's right upstairs sleeping. You here to play ball or give me the third degree?"

"*I* feel like playing some ball," PJ said, jumping off the stoop and trying to grab the ball from me. He was wearing the kind of sneakers Ty'ree'd said he was going to buy me soon's he could. When he saw me staring at them, PJ looked kind of embarrassed. That's what I liked about PJ—he wasn't a show-off.

THE PARK'S ONLY A FEW BLOCKS DOWN AND wasn't too crowded. Most of the hoops had bigger guys around them, but we found one at the edge of the park where a group of guys were leaving. I didn't realize until I got close that one of them was Aaron. He was patting a tall skinny guy on his back and laughing. I swallowed. There wasn't a single scratch on his face. He looked like he'd spent the night having a good time, not getting his butt kicked, then waiting up in some dark precinct until his brothers came to his rescue. When Aaron saw me, he stopped laughing. He was wearing a red-and-blue scarf tied around his head. Gang colors. I thought of yesterday. It seemed like forever ago that him and Newcharlie were sitting up in our room talking about who was the baddest. And all the times I got home from school to find him and Newcharlie hanging out. Like they were the two best friends in the world. Like they were brothers.

"What's up, Lala?" Aaron said to me. Some of the guys he was with kept walking. A couple turned around, I guess to see who this Lala person was.

"Nothing's up, A. What's up with you?" I felt myself starting to shake, inside where nobody but God could see it. I saw Newcharlie's surprised broken-up face and I hated Aaron. Deep.

"No thing. No thing at all. What's up with Charlie?" Some of the guys who had been walking away stopped then and turned, all of them looking at me and waiting for an answer.

PJ came up beside me. I took the ball from him and dribbled it a couple times, hoping it would hide my shaking.

"Charlie's all right," The sound of the ball was familiar. Comforting. "Say he don't need no colors to be bad. Say he got his badness inside of him."

PJ looked at me, his eyes wide. I almost smiled. I wasn't scared. Not now. Not anymore.

"What are you saying?" Aaron asked, frowning.

"Just what I'm saying."

Aaron took a step toward me, and one of the guys pulled him back. "He's just a kid," the guy said. "He don't know."

Aaron glared at me. I looked back at him. Not frowning but not smiling either. Just looking. It seemed a long time ago I wanted him to like me, to be my friend. But it didn't matter anymore. I didn't need him. Charlie didn't need him either.

The other guys started heading out of the park.

"You better watch yourself, Lala," Aaron said. "You don't know me, little boy."

He turned and caught up with the other guys. He was right. I didn't.

Me and Smitty and PJ headed over to the empty hoop. We played some one-on-one, then just shot the ball around until it was almost dark. We didn't say much to each other.

I shot the ball through the hoop again and again, trying hard not to think about Newcharlie, about his broke-looking face and that dog he'd found that time. The one that didn't make it.

EIGHTEEN

I SAID GOOD-BYE TO SMITTY AND PJ AT THE corner and headed on home. I was hungry again and thinking about the leftover chicken in the refrigerator, how I'd make myself a sandwich and maybe wash it all down with some of Ty'ree's nasty ginger ale.

Newcharlie was sitting on the stoop, holding a plastic bag filled with ice over his eye. His lip looked a little better but not much.

"Yo," I said, walking past him.

"Yo back," Newcharlie said.

I pushed the outside door open and headed up the

stairs. But halfway up I stopped. Mama was standing there, staring at me, waiting to see if I'd go back down.

I took the pictures out of my back pocket and held them out to her, but she didn't move, didn't reach for them. The hallway was dim and cool. I sat on the stair and stared at the picture of me handing her something.

"What was it, Mama?" I whispered. I felt her sit down beside me, stare at the picture over my shoulder.

"A green leaf," Mama said. "A promise."

I swallowed. "A *promise*?" And all at once I remembered: When I was little, I used to pull the leaves off trees, and every time I pulled one down, I made a promise—to get my homework in on time, to not be scared when the big guys picked on me, to get the highest score when I was playing video games, to kiss Mama before I left for school . . . I was handing her that leaf because it was some promise I was making to her. I closed my eyes and leaned back against the wall. That day me and Charlie had been fighting over who got to watch what show on TV. We'd fought all morning and then started fighting again in the afternoon. When Mama went out to visit some friend of hers, she took me with her, to make sure Charlie and me didn't fight while she was gone. On our way home she pulled a leaf off a tree and handed it to me.

Promise you won't fight with Charlie anymore, she said. *Do that for me, Lafayette.*

But I shook my head and put the leaf in my pocket. That night when me and Charlie got to fighting, Mama sent us to our room, then sat down at the dining-room table and cried. The next morning I came outside to find her sitting on the stoop. Ty'ree was taking pictures of her for some school project. Mama looked like she'd spent the whole night crying, and I hated that I'd been the reason for it. That's when I handed her the leaf and made her the promise.

I stared at the picture a long time. I could feel Mama getting up and leaving, could feel her moving away from me. When I looked up, she was walking up the stairs slowly, her body growing darker and darker until I couldn't see it anymore.

"Mama?" I whispered. But she was already gone.

I put the pictures back in my pocket and sat in the hallway, trying not to feel anything. Somewhere outside a dog was barking. *Please God, don't let that dog die. Please God, don't let Mama die. Please God, don't let my daddy die.* I put my head in my hands and listened to the words over and over. They came at me fast, then slow, hard, then gentle, loud, then soft as a whisper. *Please God . . .*

I sat listening for a long time, taking the pictures out of my pocket, then putting them back in again. "Mama," I whispered. "Mama."

I got up slowly, called Mama's name one more time, and headed back down the stairs.

The street was crowded and loud, kids running up and down the block and people sitting on stoops talking. Newcharlie was the only one sitting on our stoop.

I stood pressing myself into the doorway until Newcharlie looked over at me. He was barefoot, wearing a T-shirt that said *Everything Is Everything* and a pair of jeans.

"Your eye still hurt?"

Newcharlie shook his head and continued staring out at the block.

The day Newcharlie had burned the pictures and dropped them out the window, I had run downstairs trying to catch them. But there were only black smudges of paper left—and ashes everywhere.

"I was thinking about Aunt Cecile's house when we was at that precinct," I said.

Newcharlie looked at me.

"I like it in the summer. Like when I went this past summer, it was real nice. But I'm not gonna live there all the time."

"No one said you had to," Newcharlie said, sounding evil.

"You mess up and I have to go there," I said. "Least till Ty'ree's twenty-five. It's like we're on probation for three more years."

Newcharlie sighed and looked out over the block. "Whatever."

I felt real old when he said that, like I'd spent all my life standing in that doorway trying to get him to listen to me. My head felt heavy, and the sun was too bright in my eyes. When I closed them, Mama was there again, holding the leaf out to me.

"Last night," I said slowly, "I dreamed about that dog you tried to save, Charlie. You did everything you could. Wasn't your fault it died, you know. It was like that dog was coming to me in the night trying to tell me that."

"I don't care about some stupid dog." He pressed the ice harder against his forehead and glared out over the block.

"Yes you do. Just like we cared about Mama. Maybe not so deep, but I bet that dog took—I bet that dog . . . took ahold of your heart. And I bet it held on, didn't it?"

Newcharlie shrugged. "It was a long time ago. How

123

am I supposed to remember stupid stuff that happened a long time ago?"

"You remember."

Newcharlie sniffed but didn't say anything.

I swallowed and stared out past his head. "The thing I ain't ever tell you and Ty'ree is that Mama *did* wake up that morning. When the paramedic guys put this thing against her chest that sent electricity to her heart. They did it twice while Miss Roberts and me stood back. Miss Roberts had her arms tight around my shoulders. The first time nothing happened. But the second time Mama's eyes opened, just for a minute—maybe not even that long. They opened and her lips moved. Like she wanted to say something. But then her eyes closed—only halfway but enough for me to know she wasn't gonna open them again. She let out a breath, a high used-up sound like right before a song ends."

"Why you tell—telling me . . . now?" When I looked at Newcharlie, he was crying, gulping but not making any other sound. Tears were moving down into his mouth and dripping from his chin. He sniffed and bit his bottom lip.

" 'Cause I never said it to nobody. I been carrying

it around. Like . . . like a monkey on my back. You weren't here for me to tell it to. None of it."

I took the pictures out of my back pocket and sat down beside him. "I didn't kill her."

Newcharlie moved the plastic bag away from his eye so he could get a better look. He hadn't seen these pictures probably in years and years. I'd kept them hidden from him, afraid he'd get them and burn them up too. But now I held them out so he could see, not afraid anymore. It was like the pictures were chiseled into my brain.

"You tried to kill the memory of her," I said. "But she's too deep inside of us."

Newcharlie winced, and I wondered if it was because of his hurt eye or what I was saying. He sniffed again.

"You want to burn these, too?"

Newcharlie took the pictures from me. He stared at them. I could see his eyes filling up again, but he wiped at them with the ice bag. After a long time he handed the pictures back to me.

"I ain't gonna burn them."

"Charlie," I said, "that vet guy said you did the right thing. That dog was hit too hard."

Charlie bit his lip again and held it. He blinked hard and nodded. "It ain't the dog," he whispered. "It's just . . . it's just when that cop put those cuffs on me, it reminded me about the last time. About how that was the last time I got to see Mama living. I wish the last time had been something else. I wish it had been me sitting on the couch next to her making her laugh. I used to make her laugh all the time. I wish that was the way she got to remember *me*. Not with no handcuffs on.

"I should've been here," Charlie whispered, his voice breaking up. He stared down at his feet, his whole body shaking.

"She used to all the time tell me about Bayamón," I said. "About what it was like there when she was a little girl—how the birds and frogs were always making noise outside her window and everything was green and warm."

Charlie smiled. It was real tiny but I could see it.

"*El Coquí*," he whispered. "That was the frog she used to talk about. Remember that song? *El Coquí, el Coquí, el Coquí.*"

He sang a little bit of the Spanish part. Charlie knew more Spanish than me and Ty'ree 'cause he used to beg Mama to speak to him in Spanish. He said it was so he could rap to Puerto Rican and Dominican girls, but I knew it was 'cause he loved listening to Mama speak it.

He stopped singing and stared down at his feet again. "She used to all the time say we was gonna get back there someday," he whispered. "All four of us . . . on a plane to Bayamón."

"We never had the money though."

"I was gonna get us tickets," Charlie said. "Take us there."

"To Bayamón?"

Charlie nodded. "Paradise."

I swallowed and stared out over the block. *Paradise,* I kept thinking. *Charlie wanted to take us to Paradise.*

"That why you robbed that store?"

"Yeah."

We didn't say anything for a while. Charlie took a piece of ice from the bag and started chewing on it. He held the bag out to me.

"Nah. I could make you copies of these last two pictures, Cha."

"That'd be cool."

I moved a little bit closer to him. We sat there like

that for a while, staring out over the block without saying anything. I could hear some girls singing about the man they were gonna marry. And real far away, I heard an ambulance siren. Across the street a woman was watering her window boxes, and me and Charlie watched her, watched the water drip down.

After a while I could see Ty'ree coming down the block. He was walking fast, like he had someplace important to be, but he stopped at a couple of stoops to say hi to people. Charlie wiped his eyes.

"What are y'all up to?" Ty'ree asked when he got to our stoop.

Me and Charlie shrugged. Ty'ree looked from one of us to the other and sat down on the step below ours.

"I saw your boy Aaron," Ty'ree said.

Charlie frowned. "He ain't my boy."

I wanted to ask Charlie what it was like to be in that room with all those gang guys, if he was scared when he had to fight. I stared at him, wanting to know what he was thinking when that first punch landed.

"He *was* your boy though," Ty'ree said.

"Yeah," Charlie said. "But that was a long time ago."

Yesterday, I thought. *Yesterday was a long time ago.*

"You feel like trying to catch that movie again, Laf?" Ty'ree asked.

I shrugged. "Yeah, that would be cool."

Me and him looked at Charlie.

"Some lame art film?" Charlie said, but he smiled, then winced and held the ice bag to his lip.

"Either that or sit on the stoop for the rest of the night."

Charlie leaned back against the railing and thought for a moment. The ice was melting through some holes in the plastic bag and down his arm. He wiped it on his T-shirt.

"This *is* art, though, ain't it?" he said, waving his hand over us. "Sometimes I feel like our life is one big work of art—it's everything." He stared down at his bare feet. "And nothing."

I looked at Ty'ree and raised my eyebrows. I had no idea what Charlie was talking about. Maybe something in his head got knocked loose in that gang fight.

But Ty'ree nodded. And the two of them stared out over the block like it was the most interesting thing in the world. I tried to see what they were seeing but couldn't.

"This isn't art," I said. "It's our *block*! It's our *life*."

Charlie put his arm around my shoulder. It felt

strange. Familiar strange. Good strange. I didn't want him to ever take it off. Ever. Ty'ree smiled and winked at me. I winked back. *B to B to B.*

"I saw a picture once in this gallery," Ty'ree said. "It was of this man sitting on a stoop just like we're doing now. And it was selling for like four thousand dollars."

"Shoot," Charlie said. "Somebody could take a picture of me and sell it for that much. They could take a hundred pictures of me!"

I touched my back pocket where the pictures of Mama were and didn't say anything. I would never sell them. Not for a million dollars.

Charlie and Ty'ree went back and forth talking about life and art and things that cost lots of money. I listened to them, feeling good and safe and free. The sun was almost gone now and the block was quieter. Charlie had set the plastic bag next to him, and I watched the water pool underneath it. He kept his arm around my shoulder. Maybe the moment wasn't ever gonna end.

"Mama used to say she'd buy three more of us if she was rich enough," Ty'ree said.

Charlie pulled me a little bit closer to him. After a long time had passed, he said, "What else did she use to say?"

When Ty'ree started talking, his voice was low and even, like he was reaching way back to remember. Me and Charlie leaned forward, leaned into our brother, to listen.

Acknowledgments

Thanks to the many people who helped me get this story on the page, including my very patient editor, Nancy Paulsen; my very patient friends Toshi Reagon, Catherine Gund, Teresa Calabrese, Linda Villarosa, Vicki Starr, and Michelle Adams; the women at Hedgebrook, the young men at The Connelly Juvenile Detention Center in Massachusetts. Y para mi otra familia, including my oldest friend in the world, Maria Ocasio (con recuerdos de Titi Alma).

Questions for Discussion

- Each of the three brothers is haunted by a past incident involving their parents. Describe each incident and tell how it continues to bother each of the boys. How do they each deal with what Ty'ree calls "a monkey on their back"?

- Why does Charlie act so hostile to his brothers when he returns from Rahway Home for Boys?

- Lafayette has a difficult time coping after his mother's death. How does the psychologist help?

- Although the brothers are on their own after Milagro's death, they receive some help from their Aunt Cecile. What kind of help does she provide?

- Describe Charlie's friend Aaron. How does he interact with Lafayette? Why? What kind of choices is he making about his life?

- People in the neighborhood refer to Ty'ree as "St. Ty'ree." Why has he earned that nickname?

- Lafayette has strong memories of his mother as a reader, particularly reading Toni Morrison. How does the quote "The function of freedom is to free someone else" relate to Ty'ree, Charlie, and Lafayette?

- Issues about money and poverty confront the family constantly. How did Milagro show her values concerning money? How do the boys accept or reject her feelings?

- What do you think will happen to Miracle's boys?

Turn the page for a look
at **JACQUELINE WOODSON**'s
moving story of her childhood.

Winner of the National Book Award

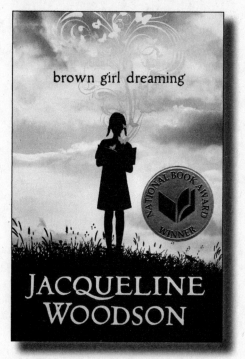

A *Kirkus Reviews* **Best Book of 2014**

"Gorgeous."   —*Vanity Fair*

"This is a book full of poems that cry out to be
learned by heart. These are poems that will, for
years to come, be stored in our bloodstream."
—*The New York Times Book Review*

"Moving and resonant . . . captivating."
—*The Wall Street Journal*

"A radiantly warm memoir." —*The Washington Post*

february 12, 1963

I am born on a Tuesday at University Hospital
Columbus, Ohio,
USA—
a country caught

between Black and White.

I am born not long from the time
or far from the place
where
my great-great-grandparents
worked the deep rich land
unfree
dawn till dusk
unpaid
drank cool water from scooped-out gourds
looked up and followed
the sky's mirrored constellation
to freedom.

I am born as the South explodes,
too many people too many years

enslaved, then emancipated
but not free, the people
who look like me
keep fighting
and marching
and getting killed
so that today—
February 12, 1963
and every day from this moment on,
brown children like me can grow up
free. Can grow up
learning and voting and walking and riding
wherever *we* want.

I am born in Ohio but
the stories of South Carolina already run
like rivers
through my veins.

second daughter's
second day on earth

My birth certificate says: Female Negro
Mother: Mary Anne Irby, 22, Negro
Father: Jack Austin Woodson, 25, Negro

In Birmingham, Alabama, Martin Luther King Jr.
   is planning a march on Washington, where
John F. Kennedy is president.
In Harlem, Malcolm X is standing on a soapbox
   talking about a revolution.

   Outside the window of University Hospital,
      snow is slowly falling. So much already
         covers this vast Ohio ground.

In Montgomery, only seven years have passed
   since Rosa Parks refused
to give up
her seat on a city bus.

   I am born brown-skinned, black-haired
         and wide-eyed.
   I am born Negro here and Colored there

and somewhere else,
the Freedom Singers have linked arms,
their protests rising into song:
Deep in my heart, I do believe
that we shall overcome someday.

and somewhere else, James Baldwin
is writing about injustice, each novel,
each essay, changing the world.

> *I do not yet know who I'll be*
> *what I'll say*
> *how I'll say it . . .*

Not even three years have passed since a brown girl
named Ruby Bridges
walked into an all-white school.
Armed guards surrounded her while hundreds
of white people spat and called her names.

She was six years old.

> *I do not know if I'll be strong like Ruby.*
> *I do not know what the world will look like*
> *when I am finally able to walk, speak, write . . .*
> Another Buckeye!
> *the nurse says to my mother.*
> *Already, I am being named for this place.*

Ohio. The Buckeye State.
My fingers curl into fists, automatically
This is the way, *my mother said,*
of every baby's hand.
I do not know if these hands will become
Malcolm's—raised and fisted
or Martin's—open and asking
or James's—curled around a pen.
I do not know if these hands will be
Rosa's
or Ruby's
gently gloved
and fiercely folded
calmly in a lap,
on a desk,
around a book,
ready
to change the world . . .

a girl named jack

Good enough name for me, my father said
the day I was born.
Don't see why
she can't have it, too.

But the women said no.
My mother first.
Then each aunt, pulling my pink blanket back
patting the crop of thick curls
tugging at my new toes
touching my cheeks.

We won't have a girl named Jack, my mother said.

And my father's sisters whispered,
A boy named Jack was bad enough.
But only so my mother could hear.
Name a girl Jack, my father said,
and she can't help but
grow up strong.
Raise her right, my father said,
and she'll make that name her own.

Name a girl Jack
and people will look at her twice, my father said.

For no good reason but to ask if her parents
were crazy, my mother said.

And back and forth it went until I was Jackie
and my father left the hospital mad.

My mother said to my aunts,
Hand me that pen, wrote
Jacqueline where it asked for a name.
Jacqueline, just in case
someone thought to drop the *ie.*

Jacqueline, just in case
I grew up and wanted something a little bit longer
and further away from
Jack.

the woodsons of ohio

My father's family
can trace their history back
to Thomas Woodson of Chillicothe, said to be
the first son
of Thomas Jefferson and Sally Hemings
some say
this isn't so but . . .

the Woodsons of Ohio know
what the Woodsons coming before them
left behind, in Bibles, in stories,
in history coming down through time

so

ask any Woodson why
you can't go down the Woodson line
without
finding
doctors and lawyers and teachers
athletes and scholars and people in government
they'll say,

We had a head start.
They'll say,
Thomas Woodson expected the best of us.
They'll lean back, lace their fingers
across their chests,
smile a smile that's older than time, say,

Well it all started back before Thomas Jefferson
Woodson of Chillicothe . . .

and they'll begin to tell our long, long story.

the ghosts of the
nelsonville house

The Woodsons are one
of the few Black families in this town, their house
is big and white and sits
on a hill.

Look up
to see them
through the high windows
inside a kitchen filled with the light
of a watery Nelsonville sun. In the parlor
a fireplace burns warmth
into the long Ohio winter.

Keep looking and it's spring again,
the light's gold now, and dancing
across the pine floors.

Once, there were so many children here
running through this house
up and down the stairs, hiding under beds
and in trunks,

sneaking into the kitchen for tiny pieces
of icebox cake, cold fried chicken,
thick slices of their mother's honey ham . . .

Once, my father was a baby here
and then he was a boy . . .

But that was a long time ago.

In the photos my grandfather is taller than everybody
and my grandmother just an inch smaller.

On the walls their children run through fields,
    play in pools,
dance in teen-filled rooms, all of them

grown up and gone now—
but wait!

Look closely:

There's Aunt Alicia, the baby girl,
curls spiraling over her shoulders, her hands
cupped around a bouquet of flowers. Only
four years old in that picture, and already,
a reader.

Beside Alicia another picture, my father, Jack,

the oldest boy.
Eight years old and mad about something
or is it someone
we cannot see?

In another picture, my uncle Woody,
baby boy
laughing and pointing
the Nelsonville house behind him and maybe
his brother at the end of his pointed finger.

My aunt Anne in her nurse's uniform,
my aunt Ada in her university sweater
Buckeye to the bone . . .

The children of Hope and Grace.

Look closely. There I am
in the furrow of Jack's brow,
in the slyness of Alicia's smile,
in the bend of Grace's hand . . .

There I am . . .

Beginning.

it'll be scary
sometimes

My great-great-grandfather on my father's side
was born free in Ohio,

1832.

Built his home and farmed his land,
then dug for coal when the farming
wasn't enough. Fought hard
in the war. His name in stone now
on the Civil War Memorial:

William J. Woodson
United States Colored Troops,
Union, Company B 5th Regt.

A long time dead but living still
among the other soldiers
on that monument in Washington, D.C.

His son was sent to Nelsonville
lived with an aunt

William Woodson
the only brown boy in an all-white school.

You'll face this in your life someday,
my mother will tell us
over and over again.
A moment when you walk into a room and

no one there is like you.

It'll be scary sometimes. But think of William Woodson
and you'll be all right.

Turn the page for a look
at **JACQUELINE WOODSON**'s
Coretta Scott King Award
Honor book

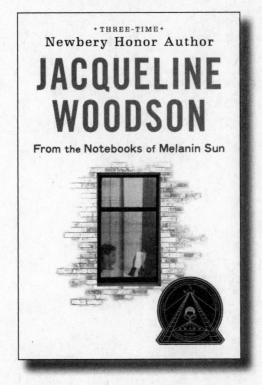

This is Brooklyn. Summer. Hot like that with a breeze coming across this block every once in a while. Not enough air to cool anybody. Just to let us know we're still alive. A whole city of us—living and kicking. Walk down any Brooklyn street and there we are. Here I am. Alive. If nothing else, Mama says, we have our lives. Who knows what she means by that.

Sometimes, I don't have words. I mean, they're in my head and they're zigzagging around, but there's all this silence in my mouth, all of this air. Maybe people think I'm dumb 'cause I'm kind of quiet and when I do talk, the words come pretty slow. Once they even put me in a slow class, but Mama shot down to that school so fast, the people who had thought up the crazy idea were probably sorry they ever thought anything. Mama says

1

it's okay to be on the quiet side—if quiet means you're listening, watching, taking it all in.

And when I can't speak it, I write it down. I wish I was different. Wish I was taller, smarter, could talk out loud the way I write things down. I wish I didn't always feel like I was on the outside looking in, like a Peeping Tom. I wish I could slam-dunk, maybe break a backboard or two. I wish my name was Donald sometimes, or even Bert or Carlos. Or something real normal, like David. But it isn't. It's Melanin. Melanin Sun. I'm almost fourteen. Five feet ten inches tall. Still growing. Today I'm wearing a striped shirt. Short sleeves. Baggy shorts. Black Pumas with a white stripe. No socks. A baseball cap turned backwards. I have tiny dreads that I keep real neat—you know—keep them nice so the girls keep coming. A pair of shades I bought on St. Mark's Place. Cost me twenty-two dollars, but they keep the sun out. Mama had a small fit talking about how we can't afford twenty-two-dollar shades. Then she tried them on. Checked herself out in the mirror. Checked me out checking her out. "Can I borrow them tonight, Mel?" It's like that in our house.

These are my notebooks. My stories. All the things I can't speak, or try to speak or remember speaking. The stuff I can't say. Secrets. Skeletons. I used to be so afraid someone would find these notebooks and blab everything. But I don't really care anymore. A part of me keeps thinking, *It don't matter.* Maybe not. I figure I should write it all down, though, the way I'd want someone to read it so that it comes from me, not secondhand and stupid. I'm not a regular boy and I'm not slow. I'm on the outside of things. I wish it didn't matter so much. But it does, doesn't it? Difference matters.

So I keep quiet. Watch. And write it all down.

IMAGINE

Imagine yourself on the corner of a city street. Maybe leaning against the lamppost there, or pausing after leapfrogging over the fire hydrant a few feet away.

Down the block, two girls sit on a third-floor fire escape, their faces pressed into its grating. Still another window, another building, a young-looking woman holds her baby up. She holds tightly to the baby. It's a long way down.

Some of the windows are boarded up. Some are hung with ragged dusty blinds. In the center of the block there is a gap where another building once stood. Flattened cans and broken bottles are strewn over the long grass pushing itself up in the lot. Right up in front, an old couch has been set on fire. Its charred remains are scattered in the lot, spilling over onto the sidewalk. Two stained mattresses *have been thrown out. Three small kids are jumping on them.*

The block grows loud with the sounds of bigger kids returning in groups and pairs, their schoolbags draped carelessly across their shoulders. The girls are laughing and teasing each other. There's Angie, the girl I'm a little bit in love with. Hey, Angie, I want to whisper. You gave me your number today because it's the last day of school and you want me to give you a call sometime. *"The summer is long," you said. "We should get together."*

Hey, Angie, I'm not like everybody else but you have to have a way to walk in this world so people don't laugh and call you soft. I can't call you right away 'cause people will start talking. But someday . . .

Angie has ribbons braided into her hair. She walks like the world belongs to her. Maybe it does.

The boys are quieter than the girls, their hands shoved deep into the pockets of their oversized jeans. There's me, a couple of steps back from everybody else. Always a bit distant, Mama says. Always a half a step to the left of everybody.

Imagine you could be two places or four or a million. Where would you be? Leaning against the lamppost watching yourself? Trying hard to get a hold of yourself from all the many places you are when you're almost fourteen? Where would you be?

Imagine your mother.

A woman makes her way slowly up the block. She is wearing blue pants and a white shirt, wire-rimmed glasses. A dot of a gold earring shines on the side of her nostril. The woman's name is Encanta. Encanta Cedar. EC to her friends.

Mama to me.

Mama slows as she nears our building, the third from the corner, then swings through the gate that hangs from rusted hinges and makes her way into the dim hallway. She stops for a moment, just inside, immersed in the cool, dark quiet. Slowly, from somewhere in the building, the sound of a baby's cry winds a tinny melody through her quiet. I wonder if that sound reminds Mama of me years and years ago when I was no more than a tiny crying bundle wrapped up in wool.

"Will he always be so dark?" neighbors nosed.

When Mama tells me how they always asked her this, her voice drops down, gets low and steady, like she's wishing she had had some of the answers she has now. "I hope so," she would tell them, pulling me—her baby, her small warm future—closer to her breasts.

The story is legend. Mama's legend.

"Melanin," she whispered when the doctor asked her what name should go on the birth certificate. "Melanin Sun."

Mama always talks about the strange look the doctor

gave her. About how he shook his small pale head and glanced at his nurse. About how the nurse gave a slight nod as if to say, "Don't worry, Doctor, I'll handle it." Then she turned to Mama and said, "But, Encanta, melanin is pigment—a tint, a stain. Surely you don't want this poor boy moving through this world . . . stained!"

Mama tells me how she nodded, slowly, waiting long enough after the nurse had spoken to let her know she had heard, then said softly, "Melanin is what makes him so dark, Melanin is what will make him strong. And Sun, because he looks up at me and I can see the sun right there in the center of him, shining through."

Mama's a bit corny at times. . . .

"But they'll call him Melanin," the nurse warned.

"They'll call him Mel, they'll call him Sun. . . . There'll be a hundred names for him. But he'll know who he is."

Mama climbs the stairs slowly now. Five flights to where the light trickles in from the roof, to where the floors soften into rich smooth pine. To where there is quiet. That's why she chose this apartment. Not like there was much of a choice because few people were willing to take a single mom and her dark baby son into their building.

"You planning on staying awhile?" one landlady asked, cornering Mama in the middle of the apartment she was looking at and pulling my blankets back to take a good look at me.

"I'd like to," Mama said softly, pulling me tighter to her. She was twenty then.

Maybe she was thinking about her own mother—how she had died the year before of diabetes. How she had struggled to have Mama and raise her alone after her husband walked out into the night and disappeared. Maybe Mama whispered to herself, "I want to do the right thing."

"Goodness, don't baby boys grow up to give me trouble," the landlady declared. "How come he so dark, anyway? You're brown-skinned."

Mama left without explaining. She would wait until I was old enough to do my own talking. Even then she didn't speak for me.

So many landlords said no to Mama. They wanted me to have a daddy. They wanted Mama to have a car. They wanted Mama to be older, to have more money, nicer clothes, better teeth, straighter hair.

Even then it was hard. But Mama found this place, stuck at the corner of somebody else's world—a world of first-generation West Indian and Puerto Rican people. A world of akee and pasteles, of salsa and calypso. A world where people minded their own business while minding the business of fifty other people at the same time. She found a top-floor apartment and decided this was as close to heaven as she was ever gonna get. This place nestled at the edge of Prospect Park. Calling itself Flatbush on a good day. Full of noise and music. "Qué día bonita," the old men sing on the first warm day. And I echo them, "What a pretty day." I learned the language of the other people here. "What for yuh wanna be a-doberin she?" The liquid fire of the West Indies. Mrs. Shirley's Southern, "Boy, I'll go upside your head so hard you gonna wish you was never born." The slow quiet of the old people, seated in folding chairs beneath trees that really aren't more than saplings. "Mmm mmm mmm. Now ain't that somethin' else?" My homeboy Sean got the nerve to tell me I'm not bilingual, talking about a little bit of this tongue and a little bit of that one isn't enough to put on a job application. What for da boy wanna say dat?

This block. This apartment at the top. Me and Mama sipping iced tea while the sun pours into the living room, turning us and everything around us gold. This is all anybody needs to be happy.

"Was I a good sleeping baby?" I asked on my fourth birthday. We were sitting in the dark, watching the candles melt down on the chocolate birthday cake. I took a thick scoop of frosting on my finger and missed my mouth. Mama leaned over, wiping my cheeks and chin with a napkin.

"You were the best sleeping baby in the world," she

said. "Now make a wish and blow out the candles." I wished for a red fire truck with a working horn, some Tonka cars, a Lego set, a fire hat, and a water gun.

"No guns," Mama said when I opened my presents later. "Never any guns."

But there was a fire truck, a deluxe Lego set, some Tonka cars, and a fire hat.

I remember some parts of those good times with Mama. And sometimes, when I'm remembering deep and hard, I start wishing me and Mama could go back to those easy close days when our lives were as simple as chocolate cakes and Lego sets.

Imagine.